THE BOYS OF VASELINE ALLEY

THE BOYS OF VASELINE ALLEY

True Homosexual Experiences

Robert N. Boyd

Leyland Publications
San Francisco

This book is dedicated
to the memory of
John Davidson

First edition 1994

Cover photo copyright © 1994 by Kristen Bjorn
Cover layout by Rupert Kinnard

ISBN 0-943595-47-9

Leyland Publications
P.O. Box 410690
San Francisco, CA 94141
Complete catalogue of available books is $1 ppd.

INTRODUCTION

Robert N. Boyd

Each year, more than two hundred thousand gay kids run away from home, or are kicked out by the people who are legally responsible for their welfare: parents, foster parents, guardians, etc. This number keeps growing, and there is a severe shortage of community services to help these kids. Unfortunately, too many of them are forced to turn to prostitution to avoid going cold and hungry.

In every large town or major city across this country, there is usually one certain area or district where these kids end up, irresistibly drawn by the promise of being able to earn enough money to survive from one day to the next. These shadowy areas of town are known by different slang words: the tenderloin, the meat shop, red light district, and other more individualized words, such as "the circuit" or "kiddy korner." The one that painted the most vivid image in my mind was "Vaseline Alley."

In the nineteen-twenties, America's flirtation with the automobile had turned to a full fledged love affair and back yard mechanics had sprung up all over the country. To spend a Saturday afternoon in the alleyway behind the house working on one's car became one of the country's most favorite pastimes. The phrase "gasoline alley" crept into our language and became a part of American culture. There was a comic strip by that name, a radio program, even a movie. The words conjure up the image of a warm, lazy summer afternoon with an alley full of cars with their hoods raised, beer cans sitting on fenders, and neighbors being friendly with each other.

The words "Vaseline Alley," on the other hand, paint a different sort of picture altogether. In gay culture, Vaseline is on a par with K-Y jelly as the most widely used sexual lubricant, and the rest is left to the imagination.

The kids who find themselves hustling on street corners are driven mostly by necessity; jobs for teenagers are scarce enough, as is, but for homeless kids they are practically non-existent. Kids who would be more than willing to make an honest living for themselves discover that there are no opportunities to do so. Left with no other choice, they migrate to Vaseline Alley and soon learn the tricks of the trade, whether they like it or not.

However, let us look at the other side of the coin. I've talked with several kids who truly enjoyed what they were doing. It was an exciting, unique sort of life style. Each day was an adventure; each day meant more independence; each day brought new friends or opportunities. And let's be totally honest with ourselves, teenagers are highly sexed. Their bodies are ready for the thrills, pleasures, and enjoyments of hot, passionate sex.

Let me make it plain, from the start, that I do not advocate sexual relations between adults and underage youths; but neither will I condemn the practice. At what age a person should have legal possession of his own body, and the right to make decisions regarding that ownership, is a matter which will be debated for years to come. This book takes the approach that the situation exists and it is foolishness to bury one's head in the sand and pretend that the problem can be eradicated by a simple act of legislation making it illegal for anyone over eighteen to have sex with anyone under eighteen. The numbers are arbitrary and the idea is ludicrous. But it is not the intention of this book to engage in a debate on that subject. This book is about the kids who, for whatever reasons, find themselves on street corners, renting their young bodies to survive.

I came by the material in this book in a round about manner. While working on *Boys Behind Bars* (Leyland Publications, 1992), I interviewed dozens of young men in prison. Some very interesting personal stories developed, but not all of them were pertinent to the subject of that book. I found that a lot of the young men I spoke to had other stories to tell, and that there were a lot of them who had been street hustlers before coming to prison. Resultantly, the one thing that all these stories have in common is that all of the narrators ended up in prison, for one reason or another. That circumstance, however, is not necessarily an integral part of the stories they tell. I doubt that ten percent of the kids hustling on street corners ever end up in prison. It is merely coincidental to this book because of the pool from which I drew my material.

Another common thread, but not particular to every case, is that most of these kids were runaways. In order to understand them, you must try to see their stories through their own eyes. They were forced into desperate situations and they chose the course that offered them the most hope of survival in a harsh world. Given a chance, every single one of them would have preferred to grow up in a normal, loving home. In fact, most of them went through hell and put up with things you and I wouldn't dream of tolerating before they took the drastic step of running away.

No one truly wants to be alone, especially kids. The world is far too threatening, with too many traps and pitfalls, to face all by yourself. Most of the kids in this book abruptly found themselves alone, without friends, without loved ones, without someone to turn to.

In each case, I asked the guy to give us some background about himself: where he came from, what his family life was like, what drove him to street hustling, and so on. I did not want to concentrate on the nature of prostitution, itself. I personally don't think it would be tremendously interesting or exciting to read a dozen stories about handjobs in the front seats of cars or about sucking cocks in out of the way places. Sex for money is limited in scope; there is little or no intimacy, no personal involvements, and none of the elements of a good story. Instead, I asked the guys to tell me about the most interesting experience they encountered, whether it was with a trick, a friend, a lover, a stranger, or whomever. I wanted the stories that stood out in their minds.

In several cases, those stories involve first sexual encounters. Other stories give insight into the guy's personality. Yet others show how or why the guy got out of hustling. Each story is different, even if certain aspects overlap.

All of the guys were under the age of twenty-one, because as one of the characters points out: if a man wants someone that age or older, he can go to gay bars or other pickup spots. A street hustler has a few limited years to make it. There are some few that extend their hustling livelihood beyond twenty-one, but they are rare and they usually manage to continue to look a lot younger than they really are.

This book will not tell you where to go looking, if you're interested in picking up underage kids. Except for the broadest of generalities, I avoid specifically mentioning street names, park names, or other landmarks. Vaseline Alley is a constantly changing venue; the cops get hip and run the kids off; pickups get paranoid of certain areas and start looking elsewhere; things change; times change. Vaseline Alley is as hard to pinpoint as it is to do away with it altogether.

One last note: none of the guys in this book are professional story tellers; so I took certain liberties with their narratives. Where possible, I kept the flavor and feel of their natural way of talking; but in several cases, I cleaned up some grammar and condensed certain scenes. If at times, the writing begins to sound like one person wrote it all, I apologize. I tried to keep my own personality out of the writing, but each writer has his own style which he uses even subconsciously. Rest assured, each story happened just as it was related to me.

JASON AND
THE BIRTHDAY PRESENT

While I was compiling this book, editing the stories and putting it into manuscript form for the publisher, a news story broke on one of the local TV stations. It involved the murder of a fifteen year old high school student in a quiet small town where things like that just never happened. The very next day, authorities arrested the dead boy's high school buddy and closest friend. Immediately, they announced that the boy would be tried as an adult, even though he was only sixteen years old and had no criminal or juvenile record. The entire incident got me to wondering about the arbitrary and apparently baseless way that we in modern society decide who should be considered an adult and who should not. In many states, it's illegal to have sex with the boy who is now going to be tried as an adult. Is he, or is he not, an adult? Why was he a child yesterday and an adult today? If we were to think seriously, we could learn a thing or two from mother nature. By the time nature's young reach sexual maturity, that is puberty in human terms, they are ready for everything the world has to offer. That year or two between birth and sexual maturity is when they learn how to fend for themselves, how to mate, how to achieve superiority or domination, and so on. Yet, in "civilized" human terms, we completely fail to use to the best advantage the eleven, twelve, or even thirteen years mother nature allows for us to prepare our offspring. By the time our young reach puberty, the last thing on earth they know anything about is the very nature of the marvelous changes their bodies are going through; we've been too busy "protecting" them instead of teaching them.

It's my contention that by the time a person reaches sexual maturity, he or she should be considered an adult and be entitled to all the civil and legal rights of an adult, as well the right to make a decision about what to do with his or her body. If emancipation occurred at puberty, parents would be forced to do a more thorough and complete job of teaching, training, and educating their children. Sexual frustration is the most paramount concern of the teenager in today's modern world. The mystery and secrecy surrounding sex generates misunderstandings and prejudices. Young gay men and women are the most severely affected by all of this and it's no wonder that, when they find themselves rejected by family and friends, they bolt and start searching for a better life. Most of the time, that rebellion ends them up on the streets, doing things most people never think about. Jason is just one of the millions of homeless kids who struggle from one day to the next to make enough money to survive. His parents never taught him anything about sex; he taught himself everything he knows.

How can I describe myself without coming across wrong? I'm five-eight, I weight one-fifty-five, and I'm buffed up pretty big for a kid my size. I've got a wide chest and square shoulders, which makes me look like an ad for a body building course. I've got blond hair and green eyes and dimples in my cheeks. I hated those damn dimples when I was a kid, but I found out that they make me look "cute," and looking cute helps me make money.

Five-eight ain't short, but it sure in hell ain't tall, either. But even though I usually wish I was taller, being five-eight has had its advantages. I haven't grown any since I was eighteen. I've gotten older, and wiser I guess; and I've put some hair on my chest since this happened. But aside from that, things are pretty much the same. I still manage to get by because people still think I'm "cute."

My background? Not much to tell. California. Middle class. Two brothers, one older and one younger. My dad's an aerospace engineer and my mom's a housewife. Southern California was all I knew till I was thirteen. That's when the shit hit the fan and I split the scene.

What happened? Simple. I tried seducing several of my fellow boy scouts and one of them snitched me off to his folks who, in turn, snitched me off to my folks. My dad chewed my ass, but told me I was just going through a "phase." I hung around with a lot of surfer kids and I knew better. I liked their hot bodies, and didn't give a fuck about girls.

Both my brothers and me were into surfing. I never got very

good at it, because I was mostly interested in the guys, not the waves. I was always trying to suck some guy's dick. When I first started groping guys, they thought I was just funning; but as time went on, most of them knew that I meant it. My older brother told me to quit it, because his friends were starting to tease him about his faggot brother. But I couldn't quit it. Finally, he told my dad, and the shit hit the fan.

Well, I've never been the type to give a big fuck about whether someone likes me or not. And I didn't care who knew I was gay. Like I said, I've got a good body and I was never afraid of fighting. If someone wanted to say something about me being gay, I said come on with it! Let's settle it.

But my dad didn't see things my way. He told me I was gonna have to go through therapy and a whole bunch of other bullshit. I figured, if my own dad can't accept me the way I am, fuck him, too. In his ear! I wasn't even fourteen when I got the fuck out of his house.

Growing up in Southern California, you learn real fast about certain things your folks never talk about. Like kids who sell sex for money. You also learn where this shit happens; so it didn't take me long to shag my ass over toward Hollywood and Manhattan Beach.

I figured I'd eventually get caught and taken back to my folks' house; but I never did. There's just too many of us on the streets for the authorities to find all of us. To be honest with you, I don't think my folks even put out "missing" flyers. I don't think they gave much of a fuck what happened to me. I think they were glad to be able to sweep their gay son under some figurative rug.

When I hit the Vaseline Alley circuit, I was one of the youngest kids out there. Not *the youngest*, mind you—there were lots of kids even younger than me, believe it or not. I mean, I saw kids who should have been in grammar school; their moms should have been wiping their noses for them. But I was young enough, on the one hand, and old enough on the other hand, to find myself in hot demand.

When you're thirteen, and ain't got a feather on you, you're hot. My innocent little face made cars skid to a halt when they saw me. At some corners, I had them backed up ten deep, waiting to see if I was available.

During the three years I spent hustling in Southern California, I saw it all. And I did it all. I did things I still find it hard to believe are possible. This story isn't about all that stuff; but I just want to make sure that you understand that I acquired a lot of experience before moving on to Las Vegas.

I don't know exactly why I picked Vegas. I guess I was just getting tired of the whole sick street scene in Los Angeles. I mean, you can't believe the bullshit a kid has to put up with when he's on the streets. It's not all fun and games, with hot sex and hot bodies. There's a lot of scam artists out there who'd just as soon fuck a kid out of a quarter as cut his heart out.

I needed something new; so one day someone said something about Las Vegas, and I said to myself: that's the place.

Vegas was nothing like L.A. There's not as many gays in Vegas as you would think. They're there, all right; just not quite so much out in the open. It took me awhile to figure out where was the best place to hustle my ass. I started on the famous Las Vegas Strip, but didn't have a lot of luck. Everyone who picked me up thought I was just hitchhiking.

Downtown Vegas, what they call "Glitter Gulch," with all the neon lights, which make it as bright as day during the middle of the night, wasn't much better than the strip. People go to Vegas to gamble, not to pick up boys.

I stumbled onto hustler's corner by accident. I was just walking along Fremont Street, a few blocks away from downtown, when I noticed a good looking kid standing next to a bus stop near a small casino. The guy was a real fox and I thought about making a pass at him, not knowing at first that he was hustling. It was a warm high desert evening and the kid was wearing cut off jeans, a torn T-shirt, and sneakers without socks. You could see his belly button on a flat stomach; a tiny trail of dark hair sneaked down into his cut-offs, and I wanted my tongue to travel that path. His nips showed through his T-shirt, even though it wasn't that tight. You could see that he had a nice body. Not overly big, but not skinny. I wanted to have sex with him.

It doesn't take long for street-smart kids to pick up on what's happening, and this kid and me hit it off right away. Within ten minutes, we knew what each other was after. I didn't care, though, if we both got tricks that night and got worn out, I still wanted to have sex with him; so I asked him to meet me the next day inside the casino for breakfast. He agreed and two minutes later was leaning through the passenger window of a late model sedan, talking to the guy inside. Only ten minutes later, I was doing the same thing.

After that, things went pretty good for me in Vegas. The kid and I became good friends (his name was Todd) and we frequently worked hustler's corner together. About half a dozen times, we got picked up together for three-ways and four-ways. There was probably about ten or fifteen different guys that worked the corner at different times of day and night, but I think I can safely say that Todd and I were the best looking and had the sexiest bodies. Todd even got picked up one night by a cocktail waitress. He turned the trick, but told me later that all it did for him was to prove that he could never go straight.

One night, I got picked up by a guy in his late twenties named Paul, a pit boss at one of the strip casinos. He was nice looking, even though he never got any sun because he worked graveyards and slept days. Paul shared an apartment with his friend, Frank. They weren't exactly lovers, even though they had a sexual relationship going on. I guess you'd call it an open relationship, because they slept with other men a lot of the time.

In fact, the first time Paul picked me up and took me to his apartment, Frank was there and the whole scene turned into a three-way. Frank was a dealer at a different hotel, and he was about two or three years younger than Paul. Not as good looking, but he had a nicer body.

One night, Paul came to hustler's corner to pick me up and he saw Todd and me talking together in front of the small casino (which is no longer there, by the way. It went out of business and eventually got torn down). Paul called me over to his car and asked me if I could arrange a four-way with the good looking kid I was talking to.

Paul's money was always good, and sometimes he managed to get "comp" tickets for free meals; so getting Todd to go along with the plan was no problem. Todd had been on the streets at least a year and he approached hustling with a professional attitude which I appreciated.

I learned early on that you've got to make your tricks feel important, not treat them like perverted child molesters. Too many inexperienced kids hit the streets with no understanding of what they're doing or why. Some of them never learn that the name of the game is satisfying the customer, not ripping him off. You've got to be honest with your customers and you've got to treat them like they're the most important people in the world. If you don't, you're not gonna get a lot of repeat business (except maybe from the types that like to be abused and mistreated—and don't get me wrong: if that's what the customer wants, that's what he gets, even from me).

Paul and Frank had become dependable, steady customers. I had to be careful to keep my distance from them, professionally; because after awhile it was like we had become friends. And that's no good. Not for business, I mean. I made sure they understood that sex was my livelihood; I never did it for free.

I didn't tell them about the thing I had going with Todd, of course. I loved having sex with Todd, and he enjoyed it with me. We just never let anyone else know that we did it together—unless it was part of an orgy situation, for which we were being paid a fair sum of money.

One night Paul picked me up and took me to his apartment where we had sex for about an hour, until he had to go to work. Afterward, I was in the shower and he was in front of the mirror, shaving. When I stepped out of the shower, he volunteered to dry me off, unable to resist feeling my body as he did so.

At one point, he said to me, "You know, Jason, I've been thinking about asking you what all you'll do, or how far you'll go, just to make money."

"Anything but fuck a pig or take a donkey dick up my ass. I'm not into bestiality. Why do you ask?"

When I pinned him down, he told me that he and Frank had a gay friend named Joe, a shift manager at one of the downtown casinos. Joe was gay, but unattached. He was not an especially attractive man; not ugly, but not good looking, and he had a bit of a flabby body. Joe's fortieth birthday was coming up and Paul and Frank had been wracking their brains trying to come up with a unique idea for a birthday present.

Frank had jokingly suggested that they take Joe down to hustler's corner and fix him up with a trick. But they knew that Joe wouldn't go for it. Like a lot of people who have never used the services of a hustler or a prostitute, Joe had always said he would never pay for sex.

People should get rid of their hang-ups about paying for sex. Some people think it's demeaning—that it suggests they are unable to find someone to go to bed with them for themselves. Not true. I've known lots of really good looking guys who have picked up hustlers simply because the hustler was sexy. Money wasn't the question—pleasure was; and most people have to pay for their pleasure, one way or the other, don't they? Movies? Drinks? Fine dining? A trip to Disneyland? A good book?

Others think that sex with a hustler is too impersonal, too cold, no feeling. I partially agree—you usually get more *feeling* than you bargained for. But isn't that what you want? If you want a lasting relationship, you don't want it with a hustler. But the absence of a relationship is what makes it so good; hot, wild, passionate, uninhibited sex! With no recriminations and no obligations or commitments.

We hustlers perform a great service and we deserve some consideration for what we do. If you want a sixteen year old, but don't think you should have to "pay for sex," if you go looking in school yards or playgrounds instead of coming to me, you're taking a chance of picking up a morals charge, which usually guarantees a trip to the joint, where the only sex you're gonna get is with someone who is definitely not sixteen years old!

Well, anyway Joe wasn't about to pick up a hustler on his own; so Paul and Frank thought that if me or Todd would be willing to turn Joe as a trick, Joe wouldn't have to pay for it himself—it would be a gift from Paul and Frank.

I said, "Sure. Why not?"

"There's more," Paul insisted.

They wanted the present to be a surprise. They would have to sneak me into Joe's apartment, with the collaboration of the apartment manager, then when he got off work on his birthday, Paul and Frank would make sure he went home after work without stopping off somewhere. I would be there waiting for him.

"No problem," I said. I could see nothing unusual in the request.

"Naked," Paul said. "Totally naked, except for a wide red ribbon wrapped around your body, like the New Year's Baby, and a big red bow covering your genitals. You'd have to parade around the apartment in nothing but a red bow until Frank and I decided to get the hell out of there so you two could get down. What say?"

"Sounds like a normal business proposition to me," I said. "I've done things even wilder than that. You'd be surprised what they can dream up in Southern California."

He looked at me with a quizzical expression. I told him I would tell him some other time.

We made a date for Joe's birthday, and Paul agreed to pick me up at ten o'clock on the night in question. Joe worked the swing shift; so he would be home shortly after midnight; but we needed some time to make preparations, and we had to be sure the manager would still be awake.

Luckily, Paul and Frank knew the manager, because they had once lived in that same apartment building. The man wasn't gay, but he was open minded and had rented to lots of gays over the years.

When the night of Joe's birthday came around, Paul picked me up at hustler's corner, as agreed. Joe's apartment was on the bottom floor; his front door was a sliding glass window which opened onto the patio, just a few feet from the shallow end of the pool. It was a garden style apartment building; the units were modern and nicely furnished.

Once inside, we went into the bedroom and I stripped out of my clothes. Again, Paul couldn't keep his hands off me. If I say so myself, I've got one of those touchable bodies; muscular and well-developed, but soft and hairless. When I see a body like mine, I, too, want to play touchy-feely.

He attended to the bow first, a round bow made like the bows on Christmas packages, about twelve inches in diameter. To attach it to my genitals, he had to wrap half-inch ribbon around my dick and balls, like a cock ring, then he pulled it tight and tied the ribbon in a slip knot. Next, he affixed the bow with scotch tape. When it came time to remove the bow, it would peel right off. I could leave the thin ribbon on my cock, if I wanted, to heighten the appearance and the feeling; or I could remove it easily by pulling on the slip knot.

The red ribbon which was intended to wrap around my body, like the New Year's Baby, went over my right shoulder and was about six inches wide. Instead of joining at the side, however, it went through my legs and joined at the top.

Paul measured the ribbon material against my body first, taking his sweet time when it came to the measurement between my legs, then cut it to size. It went from my shoulder to my crotch, between my legs, up the crack of my ass, up my back to my shoulder, then joined the front piece by a strip of tape. Another ribbon, smaller than the one which covered my cock, sat on my shoulder, holding the front and back parts of the ribbon together.

He told me I could have a beer or two from the fridge while I waited; but when the clock showed midnight, I was to go into the bedroom and wait. He would prepare Joe for a "surprise," without telling him what to expect. Paul would come and get me when the time was right.

It was interesting that Paul trusted me in someone else's house for just about an hour; but I suppose Joe didn't have anything of much value, anyway. Snooping around, though, I found out that Joe had a classical music collection. I put a recording of Swan Lake highlights on the player.

I went easy on the beer, drinking just one. At midnight, I started the Swan Lake record over again and went into the bedroom.

At fifteen after, I heard the door open and the sound of voices.

"I guess the music is part of the surprise," Paul's voice said loud enough for me to hear. "Sit down, Joe. Get him a beer, Frank."

Then Paul came into the bedroom and winked at me. He took me by the hand and led me into the living room.

Joe's face fell. Literally! I mean, his chin dropped and he gaped at me. "Oh, my God!" he gasped.

Frank handed him a beer, but he couldn't take his eyes off me. I moved toward him in a kind of dance step that I had seen in West Side Story, snapping my fingers and humping my groin. It didn't exactly fit with Swan Lake, but I managed to mesh the rhythm of the music to my dancing, and I think it came across okay.

I stood directly in front of him, gyrating my pelvis and fucking the air between us. When the music changed, I turned my back to him and sat down in his lap and ran my hands over his shoulders.

"Oh, my God!" he screamed. "You bastards!" he cried, but you could tell he was pleased with his gift. "Can I keep him? Or are you faggots gonna turn into Indian givers?"

I kissed him on the lips, and he gasped to catch his breath.

Joe was just effeminate enough to leave no room for doubt about his sexual orientation, even if you didn't know him; but not so much so that it was flamboyant. Working in a casino, he probably maintained his decorum for eight hours a day; but at home, he dropped hairpins all over the place.

He had a receding hair line, but he permed his hair and it framed his face well; it also made him look younger than he would have looked if he wore his hair straight. He had a beak of a nose and a weak chin; and like Paul, he didn't get enough sun.

Another thing a hustler has to remember is that, of the two people involved, only one of them has to look good—the hustler, himself; but you've got to try to make the customer think he's sexy, even if it takes all of your imaginative powers. To be blunt about it, people like Joe were difficult for me, at first. I'm only human; I like foxy bodies as much as the next guy. But I learned how to handle guys like Joe, and I learned that a man doesn't have to be a Greek God to be good at sex. That old expression, it's not what you got it's what you do with it, proves to be true most of the time.

For the first several minutes, Joe continued to be surprised and overwhelmed; then he warmed up to me sitting on his lap and he began to feel my body. One of the things I enjoy about hustling is being felt up. What can I say, I just like it. It feels good, unless the guy doing the feeling is coarse and rough.

He hadn't sipped his beer, yet; so I took the can from him and took a long swallow, then held it up to his lips.

"My name's Jason," I told him. "I'm your birthday present. I'm yours for the night; but at dawn, I turn into a field mouse."

"Oh, my God! He's gorgeous! Frank, bring him a beer!"

Joe was sitting at one end of the couch; I was sitting on his lap with my back toward his left side and my feet dangling past his right side. He slipped his right hand between my legs and felt my silky smooth thighs, running his hand along my left leg until his fingers were blocked by the huge bow; then he let his hand glide along the outside of my leg and around the left cheek of my ass.

"When do I get to unwrap him?" Joe asked.

Frank handed me a beer and I got off Joe's lap and lay down on the carpet right in front of him, on my stomach, but with my buns lifted slightly, so as not to crush the bow too badly. From where he was sitting, I must have appeared to be completely naked, except for a red ribbon coming out of my ass, snaking between my rounded buns, and going up my back.

"He's yours whenever you want him," Paul said in answer to Joe's question. "Frank and I will leave you two alone as soon as we're sure you're not going to keel over with a heart attack, you *forty year old* faggot! Happy Birthday."

It was almost two thirty before Paul and Frank finally left. The more anxious Joe got, the more they hung around—it seemed to me. During that time, they had several beers, but I had only one more because I didn't want to feel tipsy when it came time for sex. All three of them continued to paw me whenever they came within an arm's length, and I loved it. I've described myself as having a square chest and broad shoulders; that's true, but my muscles are firm and rounded. This happened four years ago, but even then, my muscles were nicely rounded and the surface flesh was soft to the touch.

When Paul and Frank left, promising to return at ten to take us to the Tropicana buffet for brunch, I helped Joe get undressed, down to his boxer shorts. He wouldn't let me take those off him just yet. As soon as we were alone, he became nervous and self-conscious. He went to the kitchen and brought out a bottle of scotch, which had been hidden in the back of one of the lower cabinet shelves.

"My private stash," he said conspiratorially; "will you join me?"

We toasted his birthday and I put my arms around him in a big hug. I felt his half-hard rod start to get harder, as I pressed my bow-covered groin against him. He was a couple of inches taller than me; so I pulled his head down toward mine for a long, slow kiss.

I'm not usually quite so dominant; I usually let the customer take over. But I've learned that most men fall into one of two categories: aggressive or passive; dominant or submissive; or in slangier terms: top or bottom. They are either a master or a slave;

rarely does one man play both roles. I've also learned that men have a certain sexual inclination, preferring either oral sex or anal sex. Not to say that most men don't enjoy doing it both ways; I simply mean that most of the time they have a definite preference. I usually let the customer take the lead, in order to indicate what he likes to do.

Up to that point, Joe had seemed passive, or submissive. But as soon as the scotch took hold, he came out of his shell and became aggressive. After we kissed, he asked me how the ribbon and bow were connected and when I explained it to him, he tore the ribbon from my shoulder and pulled it from between my legs, leaving me covered only by the bow.

He could no longer resist a full-fledged feel job, and he ran his hands all over my body, front and back, up and down, inside and out. He especially liked my chest and my buns. I started getting hard and the bow was lifted up by my stiffening rod.

"Looks like we don't need that, anymore," he said, removing the bow. When he saw the slip knot on the ribbon going around my cock, all he could do was smile and say, "Ooh, that looks nice!" He took my dick in his fingers and stroked it several times, slowly, gently massaging my love muscle until it was rock hard. Paul had been right: the ribbon acted like a cock ring, to a degree.

We were standing next to the dinette table and Joe was engrossed with the feel of my cock; his own was sticking through the slit of his boxers. I reached in and pulled his nuts out, fingering his dick while doing so. Erect cock and dangling balls made a nice picture, framed by the white cotton of his shorts. I sank to my knees and wrapped my mouth around his meat.

It's my observation that the one thing that didn't change much with a man's age was his cock. Unless the man was so old that it had shriveled up, or unless he was impotent and couldn't get it hard, you couldn't tell a man's age just by looking at (or sucking on) his cock.

Usually the biggest giveaway of a man's age is his stomach, because unless a man stays physically active, he'll almost always develop a middle-age spread. But I think too much emphasis is placed on the visual aspects of fat. By itself, if you can't see it and don't know what it is, fat can actually feel nice to the touch— the skin is soft and pliant, just the way we like for muscles to be.

It's my belief, and it has helped me in the hustling business, that if you can get past the mental image of always wanting the almost non-existent body-beautiful in bed with you, almost all of us have nice bodies.

He didn't let me stay on my knees for very long; he made me get up and we quickly downed another shot of scotch. He then led me into the living room and had me lie on the couch, face up. He sat next to me and quietly felt me up for at least ten minutes, avoiding too much contact with my dick. My right hand fell into his lap and I felt his legs and stomach, also avoiding his cock, for the most part.

As I've said, I love being felt up. I could spend ten hours a day under a masseur's finger tips. I enjoyed feeling Joe's delicate touch as he kneaded my pectoral muscles and felt my nips, sometimes pinching them just enough to make them sting. And my crotch is especially sensitive. Joe was quick to pick up on that fact. I like it when a man plays with my dick, lightly rubs the area between my dick and my thighs, plays with my nuts and lightly touches my ass.

When he went down on me, I took his cock firmly in my hand and stroked it long and slow. But Joe was still involved in fore-play; he licked up and down, then licked my balls and my thighs. God, I love it when they lick my thighs while holding onto my dickhead.

After another few minutes, he got up and pulled me to my feet, then led me into his bedroom. He pulled off his shorts, lay down on top of the covers, and motioned for me to join him. For several minutes, we rolled around on his bed, kissing and feeling. He began kissing down the length of my chest and stomach, and when he reached my dick he finally untied the slip-knot in the thin rib-bon. Then he eased his way into a sixty-nine position.

I was glad he did that, because for me sixty-nine is the best way to have sex. I like it, because you can both have a hard, succulent cock in your mouth at the same time; you both get feelings simultaneously; and if you do it right, you can cum at the same time.

Side by side on the soft coverlet, mouths to dicks, hands around buns, torsos rubbing hotly against each other, we sucked and sucked. His cock was just large enough to fill my mouth nicely, and his balls were large and hung low. His buns were soft, with just a light covering of fuzz.

His lips were full and thick; the suction he applied to my cock was maddeningly powerful. I knew I would have to develop a technique more like his, if I were ever to become a truly professional cock-sucker. Joe was *good* at it! His mouth felt easily as good as one of those vacuum pumps, and the sucking sensation made my whole body freak out with wild sexual responses. I even felt it in my toes!

Joe's expertise didn't stop with his mouth, though. His fingers managed to find every single one of my erogenous spots, and he especially knew how to elicit tingling sensations throughout my body by toying with my ass muscles, sometimes pressing his finger almost all the way in, but usually stopping just short of penetration.

As a hustler, though, I've learned how to hold off until the other guy is ready; so I held back until I felt that Joe was on the verge of climax.

I think he was doing the same thing, because all of a sudden the finger that had been teasing my ass muscles chose just that particular moment to plop past the sphincter and slip up into my ass, gliding over the prostate gland. When he did that, my nuts exploded. For a split second, I wished he hadn't pushed me over the edge of orgasm; but in that same instant, I felt the contraction of his cock muscles and then the hot squirt of cum into my mouth.

I grabbed hold of his nutsac and squeezed lightly while he pumped my face with his swollen cock and poured out the contents of his testicles into my throat.

My own orgasm seemed mild compared to his, except for the wild feeling of his finger up my ass. I pounded my cock into his face for a moment, then just as quickly, I was finished.

We got very little sleep that night, because Joe wanted to take full advantage of his birthday present. We lay next to each other in bed until daylight, with Joe being completely unable to resist feeling me up, and me completely unable to resist a warm, pleasant feel-job.

At about eight o'clock, we did it again, and it took almost an hour to catch a nut. But orgasm wasn't the main objective. We were just making each other feel good.

At about nine, we showered together and got hard again, but that time we were unable to go all the way. Paul and Frank showed up at ten and, to my surprise, brought Todd with them.

It seems that Todd had spent the night with Paul and Frank, in a totally hectic three-way.

When Joe saw Todd, I think he fell in love, and for a split second I felt a twinge of jealousy, but I wasn't sure why. I didn't see Joe as a threat to what Todd and I had going on; but I think I might have seen Todd as a threat to future business with Joe.

At the Trop, we had the buffet brunch, one of the best buffets in Vegas.

Joe's birthday party proved to be a turning point for me and Todd. Within a month or so, we had converted from street corner hustlers to call-boys, a safer and more lucrative way to make money. Our business expanded rapidly among the gay casino workers (and others). We got an apartment together in Joe's building and a phone put in.

Our business was very restrictive; we didn't do anybody without a referral from a trusted customer or friend. Later, I found out that the call-boy service had not been Paul's idea, or even Frank's. It had been Joe's idea, all because he liked his birthday present.

BARRY AND
THE MARINES

*When Barry initially told me this story, my reaction was déja vu.
A remarkably similar incident happened to me when I was in my
early twenties. The biggest difference between our experiences is
that Barry got paid for it; I did it just for fun. Barry is a tall, good
looking kid with sandy brown hair and slate blue eyes that look
gray in the daylight. He's definitely not skinny, but he's not muscular, either; his body is a smooth combination of lean muscle and
slowly disappearing baby fat. Actually, he's got one of those bodies that, if he isn't careful about diet and exercise, he'll find himself with an almost-impossible-to-get-rid-of spare tire by the time
he reaches forty. At the time of this story, however, he was just
out of high school and I have no doubt that his body was deli-
ciously sexy. His chest and stomach are smooth and soft, and his
fleshy thighs and even fleshier buns look good enough to eat—
especially with strawberries and cream, which although it sounds
trite, is an excellent description of his complexion, which has the
rosy glow of a boy who grew up in California's Central Valley.
He looks like an all American boy and his smile says, "I'm ready
when you are." These Marines were definitely ready and so was
Barry.*

I GREW UP in Delano, California, and if you know where that
is, you might even know who I am. I was pretty popular in
school—which is one of the reasons I left. Everyone knew me,
which meant that I couldn't be myself.

My popularity would have dissolved faster than a drop of water
on a hot sidewalk in the middle of July, if I had told anyone in
Delano that I was gay. Nobody's gay in Delano! Or if he is, he's
like me and gets the hell out of there as soon as he can.

Right after graduation, I lit out. I told everyone I was going to
hitch hike across the country, which was only partially true. When
I lit out, I didn't know that I was going to become a hustler; I just

knew I had to find others like me. I'd had sex with a cousin of mine, when we were fourteen or fifteen, but that was my only sexual experience with another guy. I'd had sex with a couple of girls in school, but that only convinced me that I was gay and that I had to find other guys to have sex with.

Los Angeles naturally came to mind; so when I left Delano, I headed south on Highway 99. To this day, I still don't know how I missed Los Angeles, or how I got as far as Palm Springs, but I just hitched the rides and went wherever they took me.

The second ride I got was with this travelling salesman who offered me ten bucks if I'd let him suck my dick. "Hell, yes!" I told him. And for ten more, I'd even suck his dick.

That was my first trick. Twenty bucks in about fifteen minutes was easy money! Especially when you consider that I like sucking cock in the first place and I like getting my own cock sucked in the second place.

After that, I kept getting sex offers from practically every other guy that picked me up. I stuck to twenty bucks a trick, because I didn't think they'd pay any more than that, and by the time I ended up in Palm Springs, I had more than a hundred bucks on me.

Somewhere near Palm Springs, there's a Marine base. I'm not sure exactly where it's at, and I sure in hell don't remember how I came to be hitch hiking so close to it; but the evening of my second day away from Delano, I got picked up by two Marines.

When they pulled over, the passenger got out to let me in, forcing me to sit in the middle. They were both in uniform, which is how I knew they were Marines, and they were both good looking guys in their early twenties. The one in the passenger seat was especially handsome. He had soft blue eyes and a deep, dark tan. He reminded me of one of the guys on my high school football team—the sexiest guy in school. The driver introduced himself as Dennis; the passenger's name was Phillip.

Dennis asked me where I was going and I told them, "Nowhere special, just out thumbing." Phillip said they were on weekend pass and they had a friend who had a place in the desert, not far from where we were.

Phillip put his hand on my thigh, gave it a little squeeze, and said they were going to party all weekend long at their friend's place. He said it was miles from nowhere, with no neighbors and no one to bother them. He said they sunbathed in the nude and swam in the nude and "did everything in the nude"; he said it was great. Then he asked me if I wanted to party with them.

I had no intention of partying with a bunch of naked guys and girls. I wanted guys, without the girls! They hadn't said there would be girls, I just assumed there would be. So, I told them, "I don't feel like partying. I was thinking about going to Los Angeles."

Dennis told me I was headed in the wrong direction for Los Angeles.

Phillip took his hand off my leg and said, "Oh, I thought you were standing at that spot in the road for a special reason."

I didn't know what he meant. He went on to say, "That's where we usually pick up guys who want to party. It's a well known pick up spot around here."

I still didn't know what he meant, but I was beginning to get the idea. Dennis said, "We call it *Bung Ho Alley.*"

Phillip added, "Our Company Sergeant is an old bachelor and he likes to party with the young hustlers who hang out on *Bung Ho Alley.* Sorry if we mistook you for one of the hustlers, kid. We gotta let you off and go back and try to pick up a guy who likes to party with other guys. You know what we mean?"

"That puts a different light on things," I told them. "I'm new at this. When I saw your uniforms, I didn't think you guys fucked around with other guys. Let's party!"

"We'll give you fifty bucks a night, as long as you party hearty," said Dennis. "I mean, no holds barred. Just get naked and live it up. All you can drink, all you can eat, and all the sex you can handle. Fifty bucks a night. Friday night and Saturday night."

A hundred bucks for the weekend? Plus all I could eat and drink? Sounded great to me! My cock was already getting hard just thinking about sucking Phillip's cock and watching him walk around naked.

The Sarge's place was a small two bedroom ranch style stucco house on about fifty acres of desert land. It was landscaped with cactus, yucca plants, Joshua trees, mesquites, and other desert plants. The pool in the back yard was almost Olympic size, rectangular in shape, deep at one end, and shallow at the other. The lawn furniture was either wicker or bamboo covered with white canvas mesh, so as not to burn you when you sat down.

The Sarge, himself, was a tall, suntanned man in his forties. He was good looking and well built, with a hairy chest and muscular arms and legs. When we got there, dusk had already fallen and the lights were on around the pool. The Sarge was wearing nothing but a skimpy bathing suit that looked like a string bikini. His cock over-filled the pouch, and there was no way to fake a bulge like that. The Sarge was well endowed!

Next to a table with an umbrella top there was an ice chest filled with cold beer. Sarge told us to help ourselves. "If you prefer, there's a case of red burgundy in the kitchen. Cold wine goes great on a warm summer night. We'll barbecue some steaks in about an hour or so. In the meantime, you guys go ahead and take a dip in the pool while me and Barry talk business."

Dennis and Phillip stripped naked and jumped in the pool, splashing each other and playing like kids while Sarge told me what would be expected of me for my hundred bucks. It was essentially the same thing Phillip had run down to me, except that Sarge told me he would expect me to sleep with him at night. Two or three other guys might show up over the weekend. If any of them wanted to have sex with me, Sarge would pay me extra, and it wasn't something I absolutely had to do, it was optional. Clothes, he said, were not to be worn, unless a car pulled into the private road leading from the county road, and then they were to be worn just long enough to see who was coming. "Our weekends are for sex, sex, sex. Non-stop sex until we drop. If you can't handle it, I'll have Phillip take you back to town tomorrow morning. For now, kid, get out of them clothes and cool off in the pool with Denny and Phil."

Sarge took off his bathing suit and exposed his huge cock. When he caught me looking at it, he said, "You'll get your chance at it later tonight. For now, you and the boys have fun together."

Sarge went to take care of the barbecue while I stripped and jumped into the pool. Dennis and Phillip came up to me and started feeling my buns and my dick, and rubbing me all over and letting me feel them up, while we swam or treaded water. It was a great feeling to have one guy in front of me and one guy behind me while all three of us treaded water, bumping each other with our cocks.

"Watch this," Phillip said as he glided onto his back and started doing a slow back stroke. Dennis swam between his legs and latched his mouth onto Phillip's cock, then Phillip picked up speed and pulled Dennis around the pool.

Then Dennis told me to float face down in a dead man's float. As soon as I got in position, he swam underneath me, upside down and so close our bodies almost touched. I watched his face glide past me under the water, then his muscular chest and flat stomach, then his crotch and his semi-erect cock which touched my chest and my chin as he floated past, then his legs and feet.

After awhile, I pulled myself out of the pool and sat my naked butt on the rough tiles surrounding the edge of the pool. My feet dangled in the water, and Dennis swam up to me and sucked my cock into his mouth. Phillip swam up behind him and pressed his body against him, then pushed down on his shoulders, dunking him deep into the water. He took Dennis' place on my cock. Phillip was a gorgeous young Marine, and it was like a dream having this stud suck on my dick.

We got out of the pool and drank a few more beers and groped each other while we sat around and talked. Phillip went to help the Sarge with the steaks and me and Dennis got into a sixty-nine on one of the rubber rafts from the pool.

Dennis was well built, or at least he was in good condition. He wasn't super muscular or anything, just nicely put together. He sucked a mean cock and made me cum in a very short time. Just as he was ready to shoot his load into my mouth, I caught sight of Phillip out of the corner of my eye. He smiled at me and went away.

When the steaks were done, Sarge served us large glasses of red wine. I had never tasted wine before, in my entire life, and I liked it! It wasn't sweet, but it was sweeter than the beer, and it went down smoother. The steaks were more than an inch and a half thick. Sarge really knew how to cook a piece of meat!

I found out that it wasn't cool to be gay in the Marines, and this oasis in the desert was where the Sarge could bring a few young Marines who were, in fact, gay. It was a well kept secret, despite how many people knew about it, because no one wanted to get busted out of the service, and the Sarge was careful who he brought there.

When I asked what *Bung Ho Alley* was, Dennis explained that, in the Marines, *bung* meant ass, and the word *Ho* meant something like "there it is!" *Bung Ho!* was used to mean things like, "there's some pussy" or "there's some ass." *Bung Ho Alley* was a stretch of road near the base where young guys hustled their asses. It wasn't like there was hundreds of guys doing it, though; in fact, a lot of weekends went by without them being able to pick up a hustler for the Sarge.

Before I knew it, I was getting pretty drunk. The wine was getting to me faster than I thought it would. But everyone was having a great time. At one point, I was sitting in a wicker chair, with my legs spread wide apart, sipping some wine. Phillip came up to me and crouched between my legs. He gave me a blow job like I'd never had before. He sucked on my cock with a passion, as if he was in love with the hunk of wiener that dangled between my legs. He had me moaning with pleasure, and just as I was about to cum, he seemed to sense it and he pulled away. But not too far away—he licked my nuts and my thighs, then he went back to paying attention to my dick. I was sipping on a large glass of wine all the time he was sucking my cock. It took me almost an hour to get my nut, and Phillip seemed to enjoy every minute of it.

When I was done, I wanted to suck him off, but he said there would be time for that later.

After more wine, I found myself back on the rubber raft by the side of the pool. I was pretty far gone, by then. I mean, I was drunker than a skunk. But it felt so good! Good steaks, good booze, good sex! It was like a dream come true. Phillip came over to me and lay down on top of me, rubbing our naked bodies together. My cock was soft by that time, but his was raging hard. He whispered in my ear that he wanted to fuck me. I said okay, as long as I could suck on his cock for a minute or so before he started. He agreed and I wrapped my mouth around his beautiful tube. I sat up on the raft, and he knelt in front of me, with his crotch in my face and his beautiful physique towering above my eyes.

After a few delirious minutes of sucking on his juicy shaft, I felt lightheaded and dizzy. I lay back down on the raft and turned over, flat on my stomach, with my legs spread apart. I felt him lower himself on top of me. I seem to remember him rubbing some Vaseline on my ass before he penetrated.

I don't remember much after that. I know it sounds out of line to say it, but I think I fell asleep while he was fucking me. It would be more accurate to say that I passed out, because Phillip certainly wasn't boring enough to make me fall asleep. When he was finished, he woke me by kissing me and holding me like a lover. I remember wishing that I hadn't gotten so drunk. It would have been great to enjoy his tender love making when I was sober.

Two of the Sarge's buddies from the base showed up sometime during the evening. By that time, I was blitzed out of my mind. I just barely remember them being there, but I specifically remember watching them take off their clothes. One of them was short and muscular, with blond hair and blue eyes, and I remember thinking I'd love to suck his dick. He came and sat beside me during one of my few lucid moments. He gave me some more wine and coaxed me into sucking on his dick for a few moments before I passed out again. I vaguely remember him spreading my legs and fucking me face-to-face, with my legs pushed up in the air.

The other late-comer from the base also took a turn at fucking me in the butt. It sounds like a gang-bang, but even Dennis took a turn; and sometime during the night, I woke up in Sarge's bed. He was fucking me like a wild man, but I liked it and tried to stay awake; but I passed out again while he was doing it.

The next morning, I had one hell of a hangover and my butt was sore as hell. Late in the afternoon, I took a dip in the pool and sobered up. Saturday night and Sunday turned out to be a lot more fun than Friday night, because I was sober enough to enjoy all the wild sex play in the desert.

Sunday night, Sarge gave me a hundred and fifty bucks and told me to come back anytime. I've never been back to the Sarge's oasis in the middle of the desert, but I've never forgotten it. A lot of things have happened to me since then, but I still think about Phillip. I think he would have been the perfect lover.

MONTY AND
THE MARRIED MAN

I asked Monty several times whether or not this story is true. He swears that it actually happened. It's not that the story is altogether unbelievable; it's just that it sounds like someone took an old worn out tale, about a guy who helps his son over the hurdle into manhood, and put a gay twist on it. Monty is a fresh-faced, good looking kid; he looks so young and innocent that everyone in prison asks, "What's a nice guy like you doing in a place like this?" Monty will tell you up front that he killed someone; but I guess the details are too painful. He won't talk about it. Monty has ice blue eyes and wavy platinum blond hair, which he hates, but which everyone else loves. He is deceptively slender; deceptive, in that he is also amazingly powerful. He won a few fights he was forced into. He told me he had to fight to protect his "virginity" since he was a kid in juvenile hall, where he did most of his growing up. He says, "I've lost my virginity hundreds of times, but no one ever took it from me!"

L ET'S JUST SAY that I didn't run away from home, home ran away from me. I was only five when my folks ditched me at a highway rest stop. I've never seen them since, which is just as well, because since I'm already doing time for one murder; two more wouldn't make much of a difference.

Tell me you wouldn't hold a grudge if you went into the rest stop bathroom to pee and when you came out your parents were driving away. I could see the car and I ran after it, but they didn't come back. If I live to be a hundred, I'll never forget the horrible feeling of abandonment, a feeling which can't be expressed in words, and which will never go away until or unless it can be purged by some terrible act of retribution. People like that have no right to live.

All I can say is, it made me tough. I cried myself to sleep every night for years after it happened, but then one day I just stopped.

I haven't cried since I was nine or ten. For anything.

When I was old enough to be on my own, I already knew what it was like to depend on no one but myself. Jobs are hard to find, especially for a juvenile hall graduate; so after lots of doors were slammed in my face, I turned to something that I had learned how to do at an early age: male prostitution. I've been selling my ass since I was twelve. The big boys in juvie liked my tender, sweet young ass, and after a couple of attempts to rape me, they gave up trying to fight a wild cat and they settled down to talk terms with me. Ice cream, candy, soda pops, extra desserts—coin of the realm for a kid in juvenile hall.

So in my teens I found myself on street corners, in back alleys, in parks, and in public rest rooms, making money for doing what I do best. I always liked it when there was a danger of being caught. I've been arrested a couple of times for prostitution, but I still love the rush of that flow of adrenalin when it's a close call.

A couple of tricks have tried to cheat me, but I've surprised the hell out of more than my share of sorry punks who thought they could burn me. Then, too, there are the kinky types who like S&M or bondage and that shit. I won't play that game, unless I'm in control. I'm not going to let anyone tie me up, and I'm sure in hell not going to let anyone *beat* me up.

Most of the time, though, the guys who pick up young hustlers are just out for a good time. They like sex with guys in their late teens and they have no interest in weird or kinky shit.

I've seen it all, and I've had sex with all types. The most memorable trick I ever turned, though, was one that made me stop and wonder what it might have been like if I had been allowed to grow up in a loving home with a loving family.

It was a Saturday afternoon, a time when business isn't terribly brisk. I wasn't expecting to turn any tricks, I was just hanging out, doing nothing special.

This guy pulls up to the curb in a really nice car. The guy is a fox, for a man in his early forties. He's got a nice body and looks like he just stepped out of *Gentlemen's Quarterly*. He's got wavy brown hair and deep brown eyes. He's got a tan and looks like a tennis pro. My first impression was that I was going to really enjoy this one.

He acts real nervous, like he's never picked up a hustler before.

He doesn't know what to say or how to get started. He tries acting casual, and I guess it was cruel of me to let him babble on for so long, but eventually I opened the car door and got in.

He drove around for a long time, trying to get up the nerve (I thought) to hit on me for sex.

He told me his name was Jared and that he was a married man with a son in high school. I told him I'd done it lots of times with married men; it's no big deal, I assured him. I tried to convince him that fucking a male hustler, or getting a blowjob from one, was nothing to be ashamed of. Sometimes, even a married man needs a change.

It's usually best, with people who are nervous, to put them at ease and tell them what you think they want to hear; so I was trying to make him realize that he wasn't the first married man to ever pick up a guy on a street corner. But Jared threw me a curve.

"It's not for me," he said. "I mean, I want to hire you, but not for myself."

"You want to fix me up as a blind date for someone? Does that person know what you're doing? Am I going to be the object of some practical joke? Better get someone else." I didn't like the images forming in my mind. I could foresee all sorts of problems and entanglements. I was ready to get out of the car as soon as he came to a corner.

Then he told me that it wasn't nothing like that. Jared was straight and so were all of his friends. No, he said, he wasn't planning a practical joke. He asked me to be patient with him for a few more minutes, because he was having a hard time finding the words to tell me what he wanted. I decided to just let him talk.

"I don't know if you'd be willing to do this, or not. I don't even know if I should be talking to you. Let me put it like this: my son and I used to be real close. I mean, we were really good at all that father and son stuff. But somewhere along the line, I've lost him. You probably know what it's like, being a teenager yourself. Marco, that's my son, has been going through that rebellious stage where he won't obey us any more and where he won't talk to us. It seems that all we do is fight, even though I tell myself I'm not going to let it come to that."

I started to tell him that it was probably just a phase and that he would grow out of it, but he wouldn't let me interrupt, now that he'd gotten started.

He talked for a long time about the problems he was having with Marco, and how he missed being able to do things with his son. He loved him and didn't want to lose him. But Marco wouldn't open up. He wouldn't talk; so Jared was at a loss as to how to get close to his son again.

I started to tell him I wasn't in the family counselor business, but again he wouldn't let me interrupt.

"I think I know what the real problem is. And I think Marco's afraid of it. Afraid of *it* and afraid of *me*, but I want him to know it's okay. I want him to know that I'll always love him, no matter what."

All of a sudden, I flashed on what Jared was saying. "Marco's gay, isn't he," I said bluntly. "Or at least you think he's gay. And he's afraid to tell you. You think he's afraid to come out of the closet."

"You hit the nail on the head," he said with a sigh of relief. "We've talked about going to a professional counselor or to a shrink, but Marco won't agree to anything like that. My wife and I have discussed this and we think it would be best if Marco had a friend who was gay, a friend he could talk to and confide in. It would help if that friend could also confide in his mother and me."

"Oh, no," I said. "I won't be a snitch."

He explained that he didn't mean it like that. The idea that he and his wife had come up with was to hire a male hustler for their son, the way some men take their sons to a whore house when the son reaches manhood. If Marco was gay, as they genuinely suspected, they wanted him to feel comfortable with it. They didn't want him to form any psychological complexes which would destroy his life. The male prostitute (me), would not be expected to carry information back to Jared and his wife; it would be the other way around. They wanted to use me as a conduit to their son to help him understand that his parents loved him and did not condemn him.

Jared went on to say that he was afraid the situation would worsen before Marco graduated from high school; he didn't want his son to fuck off his education because of a personal problem.

After discussing it with Jared at some length, I finally agreed to give it a try. Jared assured me he would pay me well. Money was not the object; his son's well being was. That was when I began to wonder what it would have been like to have had a loving family. Marco was a very lucky young man to have parents like that; it was going to be my job to make him learn that lesson, and face up to being gay—if he was, in fact, gay.

Jared drove me to his home in a high class neighborhood with vast expanses of manicured green lawns and acres of bushes, shrubbery, and trees. He told me his wife was away for the weekend. Marco was probably in the back yard by the pool, because when he wasn't in school, all he did was lay around.

Sitting in his car in the circular drive, Jared asked me if I had a plan.

"Let me do this my way," I suggested. "Come back at dinner time with a couple of hot pepperoni pizzas and a six pack of Pepsi."

I got out of the car, then leaned back in and added, "I won't snitch him off, but if I have any luck with him, you'll know it. You'll be able to see it."

I walked around the side of the house, thinking again how great it would be to have folks like that. I had formed a plan when talking to Jared, but as I neared the back yard, I began to have second doubts about whether or not it would work. I decided it was too late to turn back; so I rounded the back of the house and saw Marco sitting in a lawn chair next to one of those tables that have a huge party-colored parasol growing out of the middle of it.

As I approached him, he looked up at me with mild curiosity. He looked like a youthful version of his father, with wavy black hair, a Mediterranean complexion, and brooding dark eyes under heavy lids which made him seem sad and melancholy. His exquisitely shaped body wasn't muscular, and it didn't look like the statue of a Roman god, but it was solid, firm, and nicely proportioned. It was definitely a teenager's body, which was ripening into manhood with a glory that would have sparked envy in young Apollo.

Although it was only mid-April, he was richly tanned. He wore nothing but a baggy bathing suit, which made me speculate that the bronze tone of his body was interrupted by much paler flesh in that private area between his navel and upper thigh. By contrast, my own tan line was virtually non-existent, because I usually sunbathed totally nude, and when I couldn't find enough privacy, I wore nothing but a skimpy bikini.

He looked at me without saying a word as I sat down in the other chair across the table from him. He was obviously expecting me to explain my presence, but I remained silent while taking off my shoes and socks. As if it were the most natural thing in the world for me to do in that situation, I took off my shirt, then stood up and unbuttoned the top of my jeans. He drew himself up from the slouch he'd been in and watched me intently. Still, neither of us said anything.

I took off my jeans and folded them on top of my shoes. Since I don't wear shorts, I was naked and I discovered that I was getting an erection in anticipation of seducing this handsome young high school student.

The air was still and the afternoon was quiet, except for the chirping of birds and the hum of the water filter in the pool. I have to admit I was nervous; that sort of thing doesn't happen every day of the week, and Marco was bound to be perplexed by my presence and by my actions. I had to hope that I didn't spook him into doing something rash, like running for a phone and calling the cops.

"Excuse me," he said, finally. "Can I ask you what the hell you think you're doing?"

Looking him in the eyes, I walked around the table and bent down in front of him, placing my hands on his knees. "I'm a gift from a secret admirer. I'm your slave for the afternoon. Do with me what you will."

"Put your clothes back on," he said nervously. "My parents might be home any minute."

"That's been taken care of," I said as mysteriously as possible. "You and I have the whole afternoon to ourselves. No interruptions. Guaranteed."

"What's this all about? Who are you?" He sounded nervous, but I didn't detect any fear in his voice. I was certain he wasn't afraid of me; he was merely confused and caught off guard.

I slipped my hands up his thighs under his bathing suit, reaching my fingers into his crotch and discovering that his genitals were encased in a cotton pouch. He brushed at my hands, as if to ward them off, but the gesture was ineffective and I left them where they were. He asked again, "Who are you? What are you doing here?"

"I told you, I'm a gift. A very expensive gift, I might add. From someone who thinks very highly of you."

"Who?"

"I can't tell you yet." I was looking deep into his eyes, but my fingers were prying their way into the pouch that stood between me and what I was sure was more than a mouthful of delicious meat. When the fingers of my right hand took hold of his cock, he again tried to brush me away, but the twitching of his fuck-pole told me he didn't need a lot of coaxing.

He started to stand up, but I pushed him back into the chair. "Please don't leave," I whispered. "Let yourself go. Relax. Give in to what feels good."

He then went through a brief period of paranoia, where he accused me of being out to entrap him. I was able to assure him that there was no trickery involved. In the meantime, his cock was throbbing and growing bigger and thicker with each stroke of my fingers.

From inside his bathing suit, I untied the string which held it snug against his waist.

He continued to ask questions, but he no longer tried to push my hands away. I avoided giving him any answers while I tugged on his bathing suit. When I had pulled it down as far as I could go without his help, he gave in and lifted his butt off the chair. I quickly pulled the bathing suit off of him and tossed it aside. Now, we were both naked, with our bodies being slowly exposed to the April sun as the shadow from the umbrella gradually shifted away from us.

Kneeling in front of him, I bent my head into his crotch. Marco's cock was long and thick. The veins stood out in sharp relief as blood was being pumped furiously into his excited man-hood. The helmet shaped glans was shiny and purple; a tiny drop of pre-cum at the piss slit glistened in the sun. Wrapping my hand around his swollen piece of meat, my fingers didn't touch my thumb. Wiry black hair framed his delicious looking pole and covered his soft nutsac with a velvety covering of fuzz. His chest and stomach were devoid of hair, and his thighs were covered with only the slightest hint of fur. As I had suspected, his midsection was a lighter shade of brown than the rest of his body, and the contrast highlighted the fact that he was totally naked.

Holding his cock in my hand, I proceeded to lick the underside of it with my stiff tongue, causing him to squirm in the chair. When my tongue darted across the tip of his helmet, he moaned softly and I saw him close his eyes, enjoying the pleasurable sensations as they shot through his entire body from the tip of his dick.

Then I covered it with my mouth and closed my lips tightly around it. The intensity of the pressure was enough to send a shiver of excitement through his groin. He writhed in his chair as my lips and tongue sucked his pole into my mouth. He moaned again, much louder this time, and I gently squeezed his nuts with my left hand.

From somewhere in the distance, an indistinguishable noise filtered into our awareness. His eyes bolted open and he pulled his cock out of my mouth. "You swear this isn't a trick? Are you sure we're not going to get caught?"

I stood up between his legs, my rock hard cock jutting out in front of me like a proud flag staff. "Does this look like I'm playing some sort of trick on you?"

He searched my eyes for a moment, then leaned forward and took my cock in his hand. "I can't believe this is really happening?" he said in a very soft voice. "You're very good looking, whatever your name is."

"My name is Monty," I said. "I'm not nearly as handsome as you are."

He leaned even closer and put his mouth up to the head of my dick. "I've wanted something like this for a long time. Swear to me this isn't a set-up."

"I swear. The last thing I would ever want to do is to embarrass you or cause you any harm."

He put his mouth on my cock, but he didn't know how to apply enough pressure to stimulate an erotic response. He moved his mouth back and forth along my dick, and I leaned closer to him. The feel of his teeth scraping lightly against the flesh of my prick brought back memories of one of my first boyfriends. For a moment, I felt as innocent and inexperienced as Marco. It was like we were both virgins, experiencing our first sexual intimacy.

So many thoughts flooded into my mind that before I knew it, even the naive workings of Marco's mouth were urging me towards a climax. I warned him that if he didn't stop, I was going to shoot my wad.

He took his mouth away just long enough to say, "Go ahead. I want to taste your cum." Then he wrapped his lips around my cock again.

Placing my hands on the back of his head, I pumped my cock into his mouth. I started humping faster, and before I knew it I was feverishly pounding his face. The pressure of his mouth, alone, wasn't enough to take me over the edge; I needed to feel more pressure against my cock, and I found it by hammering the back of his throat with the head of my dick. He gagged, but then he recovered just as I was getting ready to shoot my load.

Then I exploded in his mouth and practically doubled over from the violence of the orgasm. He wrapped a fist around my cock to keep it from going all the way down his throat; then with his other hand, he squeezed my buns, as if it would help empty the hot sperm out of my testicles. He continued to suck on my cock, like a child sucking on its mother's tit, hoping for more milk.

At last, my contractions eased off and I felt weak in my knees. He reluctantly pulled his mouth away from my cock and looked up at me.

"Your cum tastes sweeter than mine," he said. I could only guess that at some time in his life, he had licked the cum from his hands after jacking off. "That's my first time. I wondered what it would be like."

"Did you like it?" I asked.

"Oh, yeah! I'm ready to do it again."

I told him we had all afternoon; he could do it again, later. It was his turn, which did he prefer: did he want a blow job or did he want to fuck me?

It was amazing that such a beautiful young man like him had never experienced either one. He didn't know which to pick; so I decided for him. I wanted him to fuck me on that thick, plush, green lawn beside the pool.

Looking at the size of his magnificent erection, I decided we needed to use lubricant; so I sent him into the house to find some

Vaseline. When he came back, I was lying face down on the lawn. I've never seen my own buns, except for a glimpse from an angle in a mirror; so I couldn't quite imagine what he saw; but I was fairly certain that finding a guy on his lawn, naked and willing, would turn him on.

I didn't give him any instructions; I simply let him grope his way through it. Something as natural as fucking shouldn't require a textbook.

The sun was beating down on us and it felt hot until he cast a shadow across me by crawling on top. He didn't apply any lubricant to my ass; so I assumed he smeared it on his cock, then took aim. He couldn't find my ass hole at first, and he kept poking me either too high or too low; so I stopped him while I turned over and lay flat on my back.

I raised my legs and spread them apart. Now he could plainly see the opening. He was on his knees; so I lifted my butt off the grass and watched his innocent face as he aimed his rock hard cock toward its objective.

His sensuous, thick lips were tightly set, as if he were struggling with a strenuous task. When the head of his cock slipped into my ass, he moaned with joy and parted his lips and licked them with his tongue, looking very much like a little boy tasting a delicious dessert and, at the same time, like a man who has finally gotten what he's been wanting for a very long time.

He braced himself by placing his hands on the backs of my calves; but as he drove his thick, swollen piece of fuck flesh deep into my rectum, he leaned forward and put all of his weight against my thighs. His face came closer and closer, until our lips were touching. He pressed his thick, moist lips against mine and I drove my tongue between them.

My tongue action caught him by surprise and he thrust his cock as deeply as it would go, then retracted, then slammed away again.

I sucked on his tongue, and was certain that this, too, was a new experience for him. He and I were the same age, but he was so innocent and I was so experienced. His naive inexperience was a wild thrill for me. Except for the adolescent games of pubescent boys in juvenile hall and in the orphanage, Marco was my first real virgin.

He learned quickly, and was soon picking up on my cues. He vacuumed my tongue into his mouth and sucked forcefully while he hammered away at my ass. I made a mental note to tell him later that that was how to suck cock.

I could tell that his toes were dug into the grass and that his knees were no longer touching the ground, because he was thrusting and retracting with a rhythmic in-and-out motion, which helped me to feel every inch of his cock.

My hands raced feverishly over the silky smooth flesh of his back and shoulders. Then I slid them between our two hot, sweaty bodies and found his spongy nipples. I tweaked them lightly, at first, but then applied more pressure until I was pinching them hard. With each pinch, he bit his lip and pumped harder at my ass, but he didn't complain.

He took his time working up to an orgasm, and I enjoyed every minute of it. His cock felt so thick and warm inside my rectum, slipping in and pulling out, and his kisses became more frantic. He taught himself to nibble on my neck and to bite my ears. Marco possessed the raw material of a master lover.

I'd have liked him to fuck me all afternoon, but I could tell he was rapidly reaching his climax. His breathing came faster and his panting became more audible. Soon, he was moaning and groaning as if he were in delirious pain and his strokes picked up speed.

Suddenly, he stopped pumping. He thrust his cock as deep as it would go and I felt his body jerking and writhing on top of me. I could feel his cock squirting cum into my ass. He had stopped pumping, but his bodily contractions drove his pelvis against my thighs again and again, and he kissed me with such passion that I thought he would suck my tongue clean out of my mouth. He had learned very quickly how to be an ardent love maker, and he didn't hold back.

When he wasn't sucking on my tongue, he was groaning with delight. I felt satisfied that I had made his first time a memorable experience.

He pulled his cock out of my ass, while it was still hard and throbbing. I lowered my legs to the coarse grass and felt him lower all of his weight on top of me. My hands found his sweaty buns and I toyed with his ass, using an index finger to rub the tiny little knot of muscles surrounding what I knew had to be a virgin opening.

After awhile, he rolled off of me, and I went to the table and got his towel. After wiping him off, I suggested a dip in the pool and he agreed.

We frolicked like school boys, and played with each other as if we had been friends for years. When we got out, he went into the house and brought back some sodas. We sat at the umbrella table and talked about his new experiences; then he began to ask who had sent me. After pressing me relentlessly, I finally decided it was time to get down to brass tacks.

I repeated that the person who sent me was someone who thought very highly of him and wanted only his happiness. After several assurances that his secret admirer had nothing but love for him, I told him it was his father.

"My father!" he yelled. His face flushed and turned a violent shade of red. He jumped out of his chair and screamed at me. "Jesus Christ! My father thinks I'm gay? Oh, shit! He'll kill me! He did this just to find out for sure!"

Marco was highly agitated and I had a hard time calming him down. He imagined all sorts of problems and was certain that his father was up to no good.

"I'll never be able to look him in the face! Every time I look at him, his eyes will tell me that he knows what we did out here this afternoon! He'll know we had sex together. He'll hate me for being queer! I know him; you don't! He hates queers!"

"He doesn't hate queers, Marco, and he doesn't hate *you*," I insisted. "He loves you! My God, man, can't you see it? If he wasn't motivated by love for you, he could have busted in on us at any time! If he was trying to embarrass you or humiliate you, he could have caught us in the act!"

That made him stop and think. He sat back down and listened to what I had to say.

"You've got to open up to him, Marco. God, you don't know how lucky you are to have parents that love you!" I told him about a little boy who had been abandoned at a rest stop when he was five years old; about how that boy grew up without the loving attention of parents, without a nice home, without the things that most kids take for granted. "You've got to come out of your shell of self-pity and start realizing that your mother and father love you very much and that you're one lucky son of a bitch! It took them a long time to come to grips with the fact that you're gay. That's not easy on any parent. No parent wants his child to be gay; not because they hate queers, but because they know how rough the kid's life will be because of it."

I didn't convince him in just a few minutes, but there's no sense in repeating the entire discussion. All I can say is, he finally came to the conclusion that his father's motives had not been vicious. I also convinced him that they wouldn't be unnaturally interested in what he did, sexually; no more so than any other parent. Finally, he seemed to accept the idea that his parents loved him and that they had his best interests at heart.

Then he expressed curiosity about what it was like for me, growing up like an orphan. I think the factor that influenced him the most was that my parents had just driven off and left me, cold hearted and maliciously. He wondered if I ever missed them. I told him, bluntly, that I would probably kill them if I ever ran into them. It made him think about the love his parents had given him and how lucky he truly was.

Marco had opened up to me in a way that he had never been able to do with his mother and father, and it made him realize that talking about problems was the best way to resolve them. I told him that he didn't have to tell his father what really happened between us, if he didn't feel comfortable about talking about sex. All he had to say was that we "talked."

"I'm glad you came into my life, Monty. I've never felt so free." He stood up and stretched his naked body out to the sun, as if to accentuate his newly found freedom. His body was so irresistibly sexy that I came up behind him and wrapped my arms around him. I pressed my newly aroused cock against the soft fleshiness of his naked buns and felt his cock with my right hand. It, too, had reawakened and was getting stiffer by the minute.

We had sex again. This time, it was my turn to fuck, and I relieved him of his virginity as gently as I could. He lay on his stomach and I fucked him lying down. When I finished, I rolled him over and sucked on his thick, swollen, fleshy fuckpole and brought him to a body-wracking climax.

Then we talked until the sun was low in the sky, lying next to each other on the lawn and feeling each other's smooth nudity and exploring parts of ourselves which were new to us. After a last quick dip in the pool, we went inside and showered together. We were in Marco's bedroom listening to music when Jared came home with the pizzas and Pepsis. Marco and I joined him in the kitchen.

At first, it was awkward for both of them; they dared not look at one another. I could tell that both of them were afraid of each other's reaction to what had happened that afternoon. It was up to me to break down the barrier between them before it became an iron curtain.

"I know how hard it is for parents and children to talk about sex," I said, "but let's not talk about sex, let's talk about love. Let's talk about acceptance."

Neither of them could find the right words to start with; so it was up to me to get things moving. "Okay, let's not talk about it; let's show it. Come on, give each other a hug. A long overdue hug. Talking will come later."

They stood up and cautiously looked at each other. Jared came around the table and opened his arms. Marco went to him, hesitated, then embraced his father as if they hadn't held each other in years, which I suppose is pretty close to the truth of the matter.

With tears in their eyes, they held on to each other for quite awhile. When it looked like they were going to separate, I snapped open some Pepsis and said, "Let's eat. These pizzas are getting cold, and I'm starved."

Conversation was up to me. It was too soon to expect them to act as if there had never been a chill between them. I asked Jared about his work; I asked Marco about school. Slowly, the conversation became more natural and less strained.

Before the evening was over, they had warmed up quite a bit and I knew that, even though it might be a little rough at first, they would soon be father and son again. They would never again be father and little boy; but a more mature relationship would bond them together.

When it was time for me to go, Jared offered to let me spend the night. As tempting as that offer was, I told him I didn't think it was a good idea.

Marco offered to take me downtown in his own car, and I ac-

cepted. Jared tried to pull me to one side, out of earshot of his
son, to offer me a couple of hundred dollars. The money was very
tempting, but I couldn't take it. It had started out as a business
deal, but it didn't end that way. There was no way I could accept
a fee for what I'd done. I'm not some goody two-shoes; it's just
that what I shared with Marco wasn't business. It had become a
labor of love.

On the way to town, Marco said to me, "I'm really glad you
didn't take any money from my dad. It makes me feel better about
what happened. But what you did for us has got to be worth
something. Will you come back and see us? Maybe we can make
it up to you, somehow."

"We'll see," I said, unsure of myself.

How could I *not* want to see him again? But, at the same time,
how could I allow myself to get into a relationship with a guy who
was too young to know what he wanted.

Marco would have lots of lovers in the coming years; the last
thing he needed was to fall in love with a male whore. I wanted
him to remember our intimacy as something that was shared by
two horny young guys out for a good time. No strings attached;
no commitments; no relationships.

As it turned out, I did go back to see him a couple of times after that. As a graduation present, I treated him to a threeway with
a hustler friend of mine.

As for Jared, I could never stop thinking about his mature body
and dark good looks. I seduced him one night that summer, when
Marco had gone on a camping trip with a new friend of his (gay,
of course), and while Jared's wife was off on another one of her
business trips.

When it was over, he felt guilty about what had happened. I
told him that it made us even for that afternoon with his son.
After that, I never saw them again.

SCOTT AND THE CONVENIENCE STORE CLERK

At the risk of offending him when he reads this book, I'm going to tell the truth about Scott: he is not a very good looking young man. I'm sure he'll agree with me, even though it's not a nice thing to say. Scott's face bears the scars of an acne war which he lost. His nose is perhaps too big and he has an unsightly scar over his left eye. His brown hair is rather plain, his blue eyes tend to look gray, and his teeth need work. However, his body is shaped like a classical statue by Michaelangelo! When you see him for the first time, you don't notice the acne scars or the East European nose, you see those broad, muscular shoulders and that V-shaped torso which tapers down from a wide chest to a narrow waist and slim hips. He usually wears a T-shirt, which shows his body to its best advantage. He is also well endowed, sexually, and his bulge is usually noticeable in his faded, worn jeans. He might not be a Hollywood heart throb, but he is one of the sexiest young men I've ever met. He possesses a trait which is most unusual these days: modesty. In a television commercial, a famous actor insists that confidence is sexy, but I say that modesty is even sexier—and a lot more likeable.

I'VE NEVER had a family; no parents, no brothers or sisters, no aunts or uncles. I grew up with a bunch of nuns telling me that if I was a good boy and believed in Jesus, someday a nice couple would adopt me and I would go away with them and live happily ever after. That happened to some of the kids at the orphanage, but not to me.

By the time I was fourteen, I'd had enough of the nuns and their lies and their sadistic methods of disciplining children. I'd also had my fill of bad food, brutal older kids, younger kids that whined all the time, and summer camp counselors whose only interest in us kids was either perverse or sadistic.

For example, there was one counselor who took a liking to me and made sure that we went on special hikes together, just the two of us. What we did together was lots of fun, and I liked it, because I was in puberty and I was learning to like sex more than anything else in the world. Everything would have been fine with this guy and me, except that he was so scared I was going to tell on him that he continually threatened me. His threats gave me nightmares. I was always scared to death that he was going to cut me up with a meat cleaver, like a butcher, or sell me to some devil worshippers for human sacrifice. Seriously, that's what he threatened me with. He should have known that I wouldn't have told. For one thing, I liked what we did together, and for another thing, I was more afraid of the sisters than I was of him. They never believed anything us kids said, and they'd have just beaten me for making up stories. But since this guy was making life so miserable for me, I ran away.

It wasn't easy growing up on the streets. I could tell a thousand stories about what happened to me during those years. The one thing all those stories would have in common is that everyone I ran into was always looking out for himself. No one cares about anyone else.

I suppose there are people who try to help other people, but you can usually figure that there's something in it for them, first. Community volunteers, do-gooders, and even nuns, have a personal agenda that comes before whatever else they're doing. If that sounds cynical, all I can say is: it's what I learned the hard way.

I can't tell about any of my sexual escapades before turning eighteen, but let me tell you this: everything I got, every friend I ever made, every kindness ever shown to me, all had a sexual price tag on them. I learned one very valuable lesson: I was never broke, as long as I was willing to use my body and my sex as a commodity.

But that's okay, because like I said, I like sex.

Once I learned that having a sexy body was as good as having money in my pocket, I started taking care of it. At first, I was living in a vacant lot, and I started working out with heavy rocks—curling them, bench pressing them, doing practically everything that a weight lifter does with his professional weights. I taught myself how to fight and how to defend myself. In the beginning, I lost more fights than I won, but after awhile, I won more than

I lost.

I taught myself to be paranoid from the gate, and I got suckered only once or twice before I figured out that you don't believe anybody until he proves himself. I was always suspicious, always looking over my shoulder. I never once got caught by a cop, although I had a couple of close calls.

When it came to sex, I always got my money up front, because, when I first got started using my body to get the things I needed and wanted, I got burned a few times. I was a green kid, and I couldn't believe that people who had plenty of money would stiff a kid who didn't have any. There were some people who didn't want to trust me, either, and they didn't want to pay me in advance. Tough shit! I knew I wasn't going to burn anybody; so it was up to them to either trust me or get lost.

By the time I turned eighteen, I was getting tired of having to hustle sex seven days a week, just to keep food in my stomach. I didn't always have a roof over my head, and I wasn't always successful on street corners. These hustlers who tell you they made hundreds of bucks every night are full of shit, and they know it. It might happen once in awhile, but not often enough to let a guy live the high life. Hustling your ass is hard work and not always pleasant or fun. You run into some sickos and weirdos, and you never know what's going to happen to you from one day to the next.

Turning eighteen is a major transition point in one's life, and I was thinking it was time to get a regular job. There was a recession on, and times were rough everywhere I went; so I knew it wasn't going to be easy for a kid without a high school diploma. I hitch hiked from town to town, looking for a decent job by day and hustling my ass by night. I had no luck finding a job, and was just barely making enough to eat on by selling my body.

When I arrived in this fairly large town, it was past midnight and raining. The guy who gave me the ride into town wasn't gay and he hadn't come on to me for sex; so I didn't make any money off him and I was almost broke. I think I had less than ten bucks on me.

I stood on a corner, waiting for cars to come by in the rain, but there was almost no traffic to speak of, and the few cars that passed didn't slow down. A convenience store lit up the night across the street on the opposite corner. Giving up on catching a ride, I dashed through the rain and into the warmth of the almost empty store. There was just one other customer and the store clerk.

I found the sandwiches near the microwave and nuked a submarine, then made a cup of coffee. When I went to pay for it, the other customer was gone. The clerk smiled and said something that I didn't quite understand:

"Working pretty late tonight."

I couldn't tell if it was a statement or a question, and I couldn't tell who he was talking about. I just mumbled something under my breath while I took out my wallet.

The clerk was a guy in his thirties, rather plain looking, with brown hair, brown eyes, average height and average build. He wore a red smock with a name tag on it: Chris. While I ate my sub, he talked about how the weather was hurting business.

Whose? His or mine? I wasn't sure. I got the feeling that he was talking to me as if he knew I was a hustler; but how could he have known?

I was in no hurry to get back into that rain; so I stayed and talked with him for a long time. After awhile, I found out that the street corner I had been standing on was a well known pick up spot for young hustlers. Chris just assumed that I had been standing there waiting to get picked up by customers.

I told him I was new in town and didn't know the area. He apologized for having made that assumption. I told him not to apologize, because I was, in fact, a hustler, and the information he had given me was going to be very helpful. Unless I could find a job, I was going to need to know where the local pick up spots were.

Toward dawn, the store became busier with deliveries and early bird customers. Chris eventually got so busy that I was in the way. I bought a newspaper, some donuts, and a cup of coffee to go and went back across the street. I prepared myself for a long day ahead. Mornings are almost never good times for hustlers.

I went through the want ads in the paper and was disappointed that there was nothing for an inexperienced runaway without a diploma, unless I had a bicycle and wanted a newspaper route.

I was ready to go look for an empty lot somewhere, so I could lie down and get some sleep. This old car pulls up and Chris leans over to the passenger window and asks me if I would like to crash at his place. I figured I knew what was coming, but I guessed it would be worth giving this guy a quickie blowjob to sleep in a comfortable bed.

He lived in a small, one bedroom apartment. He didn't have much and probably never would. I felt sorry for a guy like him— the best he could do was minimum wage and he would probably never get out of debt. In fact, I doubted if he even had a credit card, and I guessed that the furniture didn't belong to him, that it came with the apartment.

I was expecting him to want to jump in bed right away; instead, he made breakfast for both of us. Since it was his "nighttime," he fixed himself a drink and offered me one.

Several drinks and lots of conversation later, he gave me a choice: the bed or the couch. He explained that, although he would like to have sex with me, there were no strings attached to his offer to let me stay with him. He told me I could stay with him as long as I wanted, and we didn't have to have sex—unless I felt like it. He accepted the fact that I sold sex for money; but since he couldn't afford my fees, he wasn't going to ask.

I don't trust people, and this guy seemed too good to be real; so I decided to test him. I said I'd like to sleep in his bed, but that I didn't want to have sex with him. I figured it would start off okay, but before long he'd be coming on to me. I always sleep naked and I figured he wouldn't let me alone until we'd done it. But he fooled me.

We both climbed into bed without any clothes on, and after talking for awhile, he rolled over and went to sleep. That was strange. I knew he wanted to have sex with me, he'd said so. But he'd also said there were no strings attached and that I didn't have to have sex with him, unless I wanted to.

If felt good to fall asleep in bed next to someone I felt I could trust.

We woke up late in the afternoon. He made coffee, then took a shower. When he was done, he gave me a clean towel and told me to help myself.

He hadn't put on any clothes since getting out of bed; he walked around naked, making no big deal out of it. He had a decent enough body and his cock was a little bigger than average. In fact, he actually looked a lot better naked than he did with clothes on. I began to suspect that the "move" would come right after my shower. But again, he fooled me.

I also walked around his apartment without any clothes on. I figured I might as well get it over with. He didn't really turn me on, but I felt I owed him something for the nice way he was treating me. I wasn't going to make the first move, but whenever he decided to make his move, I was ready to give in to him.

Chris turned out to be the first person I ever met who was honest and true to his word, and who wasn't looking out for himself first and foremost. He helped me look for a legitimate job, and it was through his efforts that I found one. A job came open on the day shift at the store where he worked. The owner preferred to hire people over the age of twenty-one, because he sold beer and wine; but there were two other clerks on the day shift; so I was hired to stock shelves, clean up, change coke dispensers, and so on. If it hadn't been for Chris, the owner would not have hired me, because he had never had good luck with younger employees.

It paid minimum wage, as I suspected, but by the time I got the job, Chris and I were living together on a fairly permanent basis and I was able to help with expenses.

When we finally had sex together, it wasn't out of gratitude or obligation, it was because we both wanted it. The longer I lived with him, the more I learned to like him, and the more attractive he became to me. He always let me know how much he liked me and how much he wanted to have sex with me, but he never made a move; he never forced himself on me, nor did he ever make it uncomfortable for me.

The way it happened was unexpected by either one of us. Chris worked nights and I worked days. I was going to work just as he was getting off. I slept nights, while he was at work, and he slept days, while I was at work. That way, we had our evenings together. The last day of my first week on the job, I came home before he woke up. He was lying naked on top of the bed. I stripped out of my clothes without waking him, and then I crawled between his legs and started licking his flaccid cock.

He woke up slowly, and when he opened his eyes, I could see

the look of genuine surprise and pleasure. It made me feel good to know that I was doing something he really wanted. And I found that I really wanted it, too.

I worked him up to a climax, then felt his body shiver and contract beneath my fingers. When he was done, I lay beside him and we kissed and felt each other. Then he said he wanted to do me.

He sucked me off, making me feel good in ways I'd never felt before. It really felt good to have sex with someone for the fun and pleasure of it, instead of for the money.

Chris and I stayed together for more than a year. I eventually got a better paying job in Shipping and Receiving at a large factory, and we started saving up for a better car and for a VCR, so we could rent or buy some XXX-rated gay videos.

That's where the story ends. The rest of it is private. Except for one point, I guess. Chris got killed by a drunken driver one night on his way to work.

I never knew anyone like him before I met him. I don't think I'll ever meet anyone like him as long as I live.

GRANT AND THE CONDOM FREAK

*The word freak, as it is used in the title of this story, is not in-
tended to be derogatory. These days, freak has become a slang
for someone with an obsession or compulsion, which is how it
is meant in this case. Grant suggested the title and I frankly found
it difficult to come up with a better one. Grant is difficult to
describe, because he has one of those chameleon personalities that
seem, in some magical way, to change his appearance according
to whatever personality he has adopted at the moment. Even his
eyes seem to change color in different lights; so I can't tell you
what color they are. His hair is light brown, but it might be blond
or even red. He has a slight build, which looks like a little boy's
underdeveloped body; but when he pumps iron, the skin stretches
tighter than a drumhead over his taut little muscles and he looks
like a miniature version of a Mr. America contender. He is amazingly fast, but is deceptively slow and calculating in his movements. He is quick to anger and just as quick to laughter. His
mood swings are radical, but he never stays in one extreme or
another.*

I COME FROM one of the New England states, but I never liked
snow or cold weather. Since I was a little kid, I dreamed of
going to California and becoming a surfer; but I never got the
chance.

My mom died when I was young and I grew up with my dad,
but we never had a real father-and-son relationship. He was always too busy chasing pussy to spend any time with me. He found
out I was gay by going through my things one day and finding
some gay magazines and a couple of gay porn videos. He had a
long talk with me and suggested that all I really needed was a good
piece of ass to set me straight. I didn't have the heart to tell him
that I'd already had some of the best pieces of ass in high school—
half the guys on the fucking football team.

As small as I am, my dad wasn't much bigger than me and there was no way he could beat me in a fight; so he never tried to spank me or use physical force with me. He chose to try to make me give up being gay by using words.

They say words can't hurt you, but they can when they come from your dad. As a little kid, I worshipped the guy. I guess I still love him, even though we never speak to each other any more. As a teenager, though, harsh words from my dad hurt real bad. We had some terrible arguments and said some horrible things to each other. I remember that the last thing I ever said to him was that I hated him.

I figured he no longer loved me and didn't want me around any more; so I split. I never finished high school because of him. I got my higher education on the streets. A lot of them were hard lessons, too. I got my ass kicked lots of times and almost got killed once. I've met a lot of strange people, and I've met a lot of nice people. I've had every game imaginable played on me, and I've played one or two games, myself.

When I left home, I decided to travel light. The most I've ever owned since then has been whatever I can fit into a flight bag. I've never owned a car, I've never owned a TV, I've never bought a CD, and I've never owned more than two changes of clothes. Which makes me wonder what the hell I ever did with all the money I made hustling. I guess it was just "easy come, easy go."

From jump street, I hitched rides. I found out real quick that guys are turned on by my body. To the fatherly types, I'm like a son; to white collar types, I'm like the kid in high school that they always wanted but never got up the nerve to make a pass at.

I kept working my way west, because I wanted to eventually end up in California. I never got past Nevada, but that's another story altogether.

As a hustler, you meet all kinds of people with all kinds of fetishes and with all kinds of fantasies. I've gone with rich guys and I've gone with guys who could just barely afford my fee. I've had tricks that lasted three minutes and one that lasted a couple of weeks, and everything in between. One guy paid me to jack off while he video taped me; another guy just wanted to make a plaster cast of my cock. One guy wanted to spank me like a bad child, then after I'd been punished, he made it up to me by letting me fuck him in the ass.

Not all of my tricks were memorable; in fact, I'm sure I've forgotten most of them. The trick that always comes to mind, though, when I remember my hustling days, is the guy who insisted on using condoms. It wasn't just a safe-sex thing with him, it was a fetish. He was a freak for condoms. I'm not sure why this guy stands out in my mind, especially when there were so many others that were more exciting or some that were weirder. This guy just sticks out in my mind, because he picked me up at least twice a week for several months, until I moved on to a different city. He was definitely my steadiest customer.

The first time he picked me up (I'll call him Tony because he reminded me of someone I knew by that name), he took me to a drug store and made me go in and buy a box of Trojan-Enz. He was very specific about the brand and the type. He told me later that he liked the little bubble at the end that collected the sperm. I think he made me buy the rubbers because he thought an eighteen year old kid would get embarrassed asking for them. Not me. Nothing embarrasses me, any more.

After I bought the rubbers, he drove to a secluded spot near the river, where we were hidden from the road and surrounded by bushes.

We got in the back seat of his car and he told me to take off my shirt and pull down my pants. He did the same thing, and I saw that he had a decent body for a guy in his forties. He had a little bit of a beer belly, but not much. He had a receding hair line, but it didn't make him look like he was going bald, it just looked like he had thin hair. His chest was covered by a mat of curly black hair, which made his nipples look like pink islands in a hairy ocean.

He told me we were going to suck each other off, but that we had to wear condoms while we did it. We played with each other's cocks to get them hard. Tony had a sizeable cock. It surprised me, because I was expecting it to be average or even smaller than average. But as I took ahold of it, my hands grabbed a huge, thick, swollen cock that felt like a large Italian dry salami!

Someone once told me, "I'm not a size queen; but I do like to be impressed." Well, Tony impressed me!

As soon as he got me hard (he was already stiff as a board when he pulled his pants down), he opened one of the condom packs and fitted it over the head of my dick, then slowly rolled it down over my shaft. I've got to admit that it felt neat to have someone put a condom on my cock. As soon as it was in place, he told me to put one on him.

While I was putting the rubber on his huge cock, he was stroking mine. Whoever said that sex with a condom is like wearing a raincoat, was mistaken. It fit snug enough to feel like part of my own skin, and when Tony stroked my cock back and forth, I hardly knew the rubber was there.

Tony commented that he liked my smooth body. It seems to me that for the most part, hairy guys like smooth guys and smooth guys like hairy guys. I always wished I could grow some hair on my chest, but I think I'll be hairless for the rest of my life. Even my dad can't seem to grow any chest hair. Maybe it's hereditary. Tony had a beautiful chest full of hair, and even the hair around his cock was curly—curlier than most, I mean. Another thing I observed during my hustling years was that the older a guy gets, the less curly his pubic hairs get.

With our condoms in place, Tony bent over me and began to nibble on my tits and down along the front of my body. It felt wild, the way he used his teeth to bite without hurting. The little bites were tantalizing and exciting. I learned how to do that from him, and I do it to all the guys I have sex with, now. It drives them wild!

When he got to my dick, he went around it and licked my nuts for awhile, then finally wrapped his mouth over the rubber encased shaft. It felt really neat, because he was able to bite the tip of my prick without hurting. The condom acted like a protector and an exciter at the same time.

He sucked on my dick through the latex covering and toyed with my balls at the same time. He was a damned good cock sucker and it didn't take me long to get a nut. It felt wild to feel my cum squirting into the little sac at the tip of the condom. It was as if the rubber made me more aware of the squirting and shooting sensations as the hot jizz raced through my sperm ducts.

When I was finished, he struck a match and told me to look at the tip of the condom. I guess it was neat to see the creamy white sperm trapped in the latex bubble at the head of my cock, if you like that sort of thing. I'll admit that it was a little bit of a turn on, but it wasn't the sort of thing that would drive me wild with sexual frenzy.

He told me to leave the condom on while I sucked him off. He asked me if I could cum twice, but I said it would take a few hours before that could happen.

I went down on him and wrapped my lips around his huge piece of meat. I was unable to take all of it, but that didn't matter to him, because all he needed was for me to stimulate the head of it. He said it was rare that anyone could ever take it all the way, and over the years he had learned that most of the sensation was in the mushroom-shaped cap. So, I felt his chest and ran my hands through his thick curly hair while sucking on his swollen shaft.

I hardly noticed the condom, except for the loose flap at the tip, the part that catches the jizz. In fact, the latex rubber made it feel super slick when I held on to it, which I had to do when he started shooting his wad. If I hadn't held onto his shaft, he would have rammed it down my throat! When he hit his orgasm, he grabbed me by the back of the head and held me in place while he tried to make me deep-throat that power driver of his. What he had said earlier about no one taking it all the way didn't seem to make any difference when he reached his climax and exploded with a load of hot cum.

When he was done, he felt my cock and discovered that I was still hard. It had been exciting to feel his huge cock in my mouth and, instead of going soft, my cock stayed rock hard. He asked me again if I could get off twice, but I told him that there was just no way I could shoot my load a second time without recuperating first.

Before removing the condom from my dick, Tony wanted to wait until it went soft. To remove a condom from a stiff cock, you've got to roll it back the way it was when you took it out of the pack; but if you wait till it's soft, it can slide right off. Tony wanted to be able to take it off without having to re-roll it. He told me that he would save it for a few days before throwing it away.

I asked him to tell me the truth: did he drink the cum, later? But he wouldn't tell me. I can't see any other reason for keeping it, and I even accused him of putting it in the freezer to make a popsicle out of it. He jokingly said that he used the whole thing as bubble gum. We laughed and joked about it every time he picked me up. I always had fun when I went with Tony, but he always insisted on using rubbers, he always saved them, and he never told me what he did with them. And I guess that's why he'll always be the trick I remember the most.

KENNY AND HIS
SURROGATE FATHER

Of all the kids in this book, Kenny is, without a doubt, the most athletic and the most "All American Boy" of the group. He's over six feet tall and built like a swimmer—long, slender lines without being overly muscular. He is quick and agile; his long neck, square shoulders, broad chest, and narrow stomach turn heads no matter how he's dressed—or undressed, as the case may be. He looks like the perfect male model for one of those home muscle-building machines. There is no doubt in my mind that many a young girl has eaten her heart out because Kenny is gay and prefers men to women. Kenny's story, however, isn't so much about his days as a hustler as it is about what can, and sometimes does, happen to a fabulously good looking street hustler when he gets discovered by someone who is willing to devote time, love, and money to the young man's future.

I GREW UP IN New England, in a well-to-do family. I had two older brothers and one younger sister. My brothers were active in school athletics and it was expected that I would follow in their footsteps. I liked sports well enough, but when I entered puberty, I found myself looking at guys, not girls, and P.E. was my favorite class, because of the naked boys in the showers, not because of athletics.

Two of the sports I participated in were swimming and basketball, but the one I preferred the most was wrestling, because I could get close to another guy's body. I'd known I was gay since I was old enough to jack off, and it didn't bother me. The only thing that bothered me was that I would have become a laughing stock if the other guys found out; so I had to be careful not to let anyone know.

One time, I got a hardon when I was wrestling with this really fantastically good looking upper classman. I'm pretty sure he noticed, but he pretended not to; he just never wrestled with me again.

In my senior year, I was wrestling with this scrawny young sophomore who suddenly developed a big hardon which I couldn't ignore, and didn't *want* to ignore. We were just practicing; so we continued to tumble with each other and we both got so hot, we were afraid that some of the other guys were going to see what was going on.

That day after school, he invited me to his house and we ended up in his bedroom. He told me his parents wouldn't be home for hours. But right when we were totally naked and wrestling around on his bed, with boners so hard they could have snapped in two, his father walked in on us! He had come home from work early and had heard us making noise. He opened the bedroom door without warning and stood there looking at us until we noticed him. He was really pissed!

I was never so embarrassed in all my life! I could have died, then and there. While running around like an idiot, trying to put my clothes on, I made the mistake of telling him the truth about who I was and where I lived.

That night, my father took me into his den and suddenly slapped my face so hard it made me fall backward. The other guy's father had called to let my dad know what he had walked in on. Well, let me tell you, my father was so straight that even the slightest hint of homosexuality on my part would have gotten me the beating of my life. After slapping me, however, he calmed down. He made me sit in the chair in front of his desk and listen to him. He wouldn't let me say a word while he ranted and raved about faggots and sissies and no son of his, and so on. He told me he had decided to send me away to military school, and he would let the dean know what my problem was. He would see to it that I got all this fucking sissy shit kicked out of me.

I knew I wouldn't be able to handle being in a school full of boys where everyone knew I was gay and where the staff would always be watching my every move; so I made the decision to run away from home before he could make good on his threat.

I hitchhiked clear across the country (and believe me, I could tell a few wild stories about what happened along the way!) I ended up in Hollywood, cold, tired, hungry. I met a lot of kids my own age who were also runaways. It's amazing how many homeless kids I ran into.

I learned real quick how to make pocket money, to keep from starving, by selling my body, and (if I say so myself) never had any problems finding guys who were willing to pay my price. I don't like to brag, but for this story I've got to tell you that I'm built pretty good and I'm not bad looking. I even ended up in an X-rated gay video, but I'm not telling which one.

Hollywood Boulevard, Sunset Boulevard, then Santa Monica Boulevard were my training grounds. I managed to learn a lot about sex, and about what makes men feel good, and I managed to keep food in my mouth and clothes on my back. But it was no kind of life for a guy who wants to make something of himself in the long run. As it turns out, I got real lucky, luckier than most, I guess.

One day, near the end of summer, I decided to try my luck on Pacific Coast Highway. Up near Santa Barbara, I got picked up by a quiet, soft-spoken businessman in a brand new Corvette. The man obviously had lots of money and it didn't take him long to let me know that he was interested in my body. When we got past the uncertainties of who wanted what and for how much, he told me he lived in Ventura and wondered if I would be interested in going home with him. He agreed to pay me an extra hundred bucks for spending the night with him, but I had to agree to do anything and everything. We then introduced ourselves. I'm going to call him Gavin for the purposes of this story, even though that wasn't his real name.

I asked if there was any kinky shit involved. He told me the only kinky stuff would involve having me dress like a school jock— you know, jock strap, letterman jacket, see-through football jerseys and so on. He told me he had a thing for high school jocks and I looked like the perfect guy to fulfill his fantasies.

Gavin's home in Ventura was in the foothills and was obviously upper middle class. He parked the Corvette in a three car garage next to a Mercedes Benz. The house itself was absolutely huge and I thought it was funny how one single guy could live in a house so big. In addition to a large, elegantly furnished living room, an even larger rec-room, a kitchen, and dining room, there were five large bedrooms, which he didn't need and which he had converted into things like a den, a guest bedroom, a workout room, a computer room, and a VCR room. The swimming pool was almost regulation size. I had never seen a pool that big in someone's back yard. When I asked him what he did for a living, all he would tell me was that he was in a high-tech field.

He asked me to strip down to my underwear while he fixed lunch. He also stripped down, so I wouldn't feel self-conscious. When I took my clothes off, he admired my body and commented that I was exactly what he had in mind. Over sandwiches and Manhandler soup, he told me he had always wanted a high school jock for a sex partner. He had not been athletically inclined in high school, but he had always wanted to take the school's quarterback to bed. He never built up the nerve to approach the guy; but since then, his sexual fantasies had always involved athletes and jocks, especially guys that looked like me.

I had turned eighteen in July of that year and my body was filling out nicely. No doubt, I could have excelled in sports if I had wanted to do more than just wrestle with sexy guys to see who would get a hardon. My body is just naturally well built. I've always been lucky that way: it doesn't matter how much or how little I eat, I manage to stay slender but never seem to lose any muscle tone.

For a man in his late thirties, and especially for a guy who claimed not to be athletically inclined, Gavin had a pretty good body. He told me he worked out with weights in his own weight room and he swam in the pool every day; but he confided in me that even a six year old beginner could probably beat him at basketball or baseball. "I don't like sports," he said, "I like athletes."

He led me into the guest bedroom and took a jock strap out of the chest of drawers and tossed it to me. He asked me to take off my underwear and slip into the jock strap. He watched me closely as I took off my shorts. I gave him a little treat by taking my time getting into the jock strap. For my age, my dick is pretty big, and most of the guys I've had sex with like it that way.

He asked me if he could feel it before I put on the jock strap. "Of course," I said, "for what you're paying me, you can feel anything you want." We both got hot and bothered while he stood right next to me and felt my dick and balls. I figured he would want me to; so I reached into his shorts and took out his dick and stroked it while he played with mine. Standing close to him, like that, I realized that Gavin was several inches shorter than me and that he was covered with an almost invisible coat of fine blond hair, so fine you had to be up close to see it. Just as I was getting ready to fall on the bed and have hot and wild sex with him, he pulled away and said, "Not yet."

He laid a pair of tennis shorts on the bed and said, "Inside the house, either go completely naked or wear nothing but that jock strap," watching me closely as I pulled the straps around my buns and tucked my swollen cock into the rib-knit pouch. "But if you have to answer the door, or go outside for any reason, put on the tennis shorts. They're just your size or maybe a little bit bigger. If they hang low on your hips, no big deal, I like it better that way. I also like the way you fill out that supporter! You and I are going to get along great."

He didn't seem to be in a hurry to have sex, though; he spent most of the afternoon talking and getting me to talk. I told him a lot, without telling him everything, and I suppose he did the same thing. We went from room to room as we talked; he showed me the weight room, with wall-to-wall tumbling mat on top of the carpet, a Soloflex machine, and a complete set of iron weights, and even a set of pulleys mounted on the outside wall. In the VCR room, he showed me a huge library of videos, everything from the Godfather trilogy to XXX-rated gay videos. There was a giant screen TV, a couple of Lazy Boy recliners, a couch, and a coffee table. (There was plenty of floor space available, just in case the videos generated more heat than the viewers could handle!) He slipped a gay video into the machine and we watched a couple of jock type studs go through the motions of stripping each other's clothes off while pretending to be engaged in a wrestling match. "Those models are fine," Gavin said, "but you're even better. I wish I had two studs just like you."

His master bedroom was the biggest room in the house, with a huge king sized bed, two walk-in closets, black marble steps leading up to an elevated bathtub, big enough for four people and containing a built in Jacuzzi. The bathroom was big enough for a sit-down desk (or makeup table, if a woman lived there) and an enclosed shower. My own folks were well off, financially, but this guy made them look like the poor people of Paris.

The computer room was the only messy room in the house. I could tell that he spent a lot of time there. I guessed that his high-tech job somehow involved computers. He told me that if I was interested in learning about computers, he would teach me; but otherwise, the computer room was off-limits. There was too much important stuff in memory, and I might fuck it off by not knowing what I'm doing.

No matter what he was doing or what he was saying, Gavin always managed to get close enough to me to feel me up. Sometimes, just a hand on my shoulder; other times, fingers in my jock strap or on my naked buns. I figured that since he was such a touchy-feely kind of guy, he probably wanted me to do the same to him; so I followed his lead and felt him up whenever it wasn't awkward. I liked him. He wasn't the pushy type and he wasn't coarse or obnoxious. Some people would call him a nerd—I did in my own mind, at first, but I didn't see him that way after I got to know him. He was intelligent without being a bore or a know-it-all, and he had a good sense of humor. I guess it's true that you can't dislike someone who likes you and admires you. In a very short time, Gavin was becoming a good friend and I saw in him the father figure that my own dad had failed at.

In the middle of the afternoon, we went swimming in the nude. His backyard provided enough privacy that no one would ever see us. Afterward, we just lay around on the deck chairs, sunbathing in the nude and drinking soft drinks. He told me I could help myself to beer or alcohol if I wanted to, but he would prefer that I didn't drink to excess. It felt really good being with him, he wasn't demanding or overbearing and I wanted time to stand still. I dreaded having to hit the bricks again the next day, and I tried not to let myself think about it but thoughts about my insecurity kept coming to mind.

Summer was coming to an end, school was getting closer, and I was beginning to feel homesick and depressed. I had never wanted to drop out of school. In fact, I had wanted to go on to college. Having run away from home had killed all my hopes and dreams for a career and a comfortable living. I wanted to have a home like Gavin's someday; maybe even a lover to share things with. I wondered what would become of me on the streets. AIDS was just making the news and I figured that if I wasn't careful who

I had sex with I would probably die of that horrible disease before I reached twenty.

Looking at Gavin, his naked body sprawled casually on a deck chair, the late August sun glinting off his tanned skin, I made the assumption that he was fairly healthy. I couldn't understand why he wasn't athletic. His body was small and compact, muscular and well-defined. I don't think his poor performance at sports was a lack of natural ability, I think it was a lack of self-confidence. He proved to be a good swimmer and, later on, he even proved to be agile in bed. I think being awkward when he was in the company of an athlete was just an integral part of his fantasy.

Most of the time, when I was just turning tricks, I didn't get excited over the guys I was having sex with. Sex had usually been quick hand jobs or blow jobs in the front seats of cars; once in awhile, it was a quick fling in a motel room or in some guy's sleazy apartment. Nine times out of ten, I didn't even get a hardon unless the guy beat me off or wanted me to fuck him, and even then it was all I could do to get it stiff and keep it that way long enough to penetrate. With Gavin, on the other hand, I knew I wasn't going to have that problem. Every time we touched each other that afternoon, I instantly got hard.

Around five o'clock, we went inside and climbed into the black marble tub. Gavin turned on the Jacuzzi and we enjoyed a half hour of sex play while the waters swarmed all around us like a liquid massage. We kept getting each other so hot that we had to back off before catching a nut. The whole afternoon had been one erotic foreplay session.

We crawled out of the tub just in time, because I think if he had touched my swollen cock one more time I would have exploded all over him. He was feeling just as hot; so he insisted that we take cold showers before dinner.

We ate in silk black pajama bottoms and satin smoking jackets—his only exception to the jock-strap or naked rule. He served a sweet sherry wine for dessert and after several glasses, I was starting to get high.

After dinner, he put a video in the VCR; it was called "The Beast Master." He told me it was his favorite video. I fell in love with Mark Singer, then and there; and to this day, "The Beast Master" is also one of my own favorites.

He then put a gay video in the machine and we watched twelve different hunks romp with each other in studio and outdoor settings. I didn't need the additional visual stimulation to make me feel horny; Mark Singer had already got me hot and I was just waiting for Gavin to call the shots. After the videos, and after one more glass of sherry, by which time I was feeling good and fuzzy, he suggested a tumble on the mat in the weight room.

I got up to leave the VCR room, but he stopped me and deliberately took a long time helping me out of the smoking jacket and pajamas. When the black silk fell to the floor, my cock was raging with an erection. Gavin knew how to use his hands in ways that couldn't help but stimulate sexual arousal, even doing something simple like untying the pajama strings. Without being gross or disgusting, he could gently brush against my cock or run a fingernail through my pubic hairs in a way that seemed almost innocent and unplanned. I had expected him to try to kiss me; but when he didn't, I decided to surprise him and be the one to initiate the kiss.

I was totally naked and he still had on his smoking jacket and pajamas, but I wrapped my arms around him and bent my face down to his and lightly brushed my lips across his. I could tell that I caught him by surprise, but he gave in to me and let me do whatever I wanted to do. So, I pressed our lips together, while rubbing my hard dick into his silk covered groin. Then I pried his lips apart and sucked on his tongue, which definitely created a response between his legs. His cock poked against the silk material, as if trying to lower the barrier between our raging cocks. Sucking on his tongue, I reached down and untied the pajama string with as light a touch as I could manage, trying to do it the sexy way he did it.

When the pajamas fell to the floor, I moved my hand under his smoking jacket and ran my fingers through the fine silky hair of his stomach and chest. I didn't have any fingernails; so I couldn't lightly scratch his nuts the way he did mine.

For a long time, we felt up each other's swollen, throbbing hardons, lightly squeezing the rubbery heads and then touching each other's nuts so softly it almost tickled, but sent sparks of electricity through our bodies. By now, my nuts were aching and his feather-like touch gave me such intense pleasure that my whole body trembled and I felt weak.

He pulled away from me and told me to go get my jock strap and to meet him in the weight room.

I found the jock strap in the guest bedroom, took my time getting into it, feeling the nakedness of my own body and the skimpiness of the elastic pouch and straps. I went into the weight room and worked out with the pulleys while waiting for Gavin. When he came in, he was wearing an abbreviated wrestler's uniform, but it looked more like what we call a slingshot—two thin straps led away from a small pouch, up over the shoulders and down the back into the crack of his ass to join again at the base of the pouch.

"I'll bet I can flip you and dick you before you can throw me and blow me," he challenged me.

"I'm bigger than you," I said, for lack of anything better to say. I didn't know if Gavin was the type to act out his fantasies with role playing and game playing, or if he was just getting in the mood.

"The bigger they are, the harder they fall." He looked directly at my crotch, then said, "And it looks as if you're about as big as they come. In fact, I'd like to see that big thing of yours cum! On your knees, jock! Let's see if you're as hot as you look."

I went to the middle of the room and knelt on the mat in the starting position for a wrestling match. Gavin knelt beside me, ran his hands over my buns and down my thighs, then back up again between my legs and pulled on the elastic material where the straps join the pouch, giving it a little snap; then he put his left hand at my left elbow and wrapped his right arm around my waist.

"On three," he said. "One. Two. Three." He quickly tried to pull my arm out from under me, but I kicked out with my legs and rolled back on top of him. He didn't fall for it; he scooted forward, still holding tight to my left arm. We went round in circles a couple of times, our semi-nude bodies rubbing and bumping, my bare feet sometimes slipping on the mat.

Gavin was stronger than he looked and more agile than he had claimed to be.

Seeing that our circular motion was getting us nowhere, I abruptly put on the brakes and spun in the opposite direction, catching him off guard just long enough to free my left arm. In a flash, I was on top of him, my cock rubbing against his bare buns through the pouch of the jock strap. I had my right arm wrapped under his and my hand wrapped around his neck. Using all of my strength, I whirled him over and around underneath me, almost pinning his shoulders.

He arched his left shoulder off the mat, and I lay on top of him, using my body as a dead weight, our cocks jabbing each other and our legs locked in an erotic dance of their own. My elbows locked and I pressed down in his shoulders, pinning him.

"One. Two. Three." I counted him out.

"Two falls out of three," he insisted.

That was fine with me, because I was enjoying playing with his almost naked body, especially now that he and I were starting to perspire from the exertion. Before letting him up, I lifted my weight off of him, but then sat down on him again, straddling his stomach. Holding him down, I pinched both of his nips, gently at first, then harder. Gavin's face was a mask of intense pleasure, his eyelids lowered and his tongue lightly licking his lips. He reached up, apparently to pinch my tits, but I snapped the elastic shoulder straps, just as he had done to my supporter straps. It wouldn't have stung, except that my weight on him created an unexpected tension. The slight sting caused him to open his eyes. He smiled at me. "You bastard," he whispered. He quickly reached for my cock, as if to injure me, but I jumped back and rose to my feet.

The next two falls went pretty much the same way, except that I purposely let him win the second fall, in order to have the third one.

During the third fall, though, I deliberately pulled one of his sling shot straps off his right shoulder. "Are you going to wrestle in a strapless gown?" I kidded him, reaching for the other strap.

We got away from our wrestling match while we fought for control of his left strap. We stood up at one point and went round and round like two sumo wrestlers trying to gain the best advantage. Then, I let him grab me, just as I let my feet give out from under me. I dragged him down on top of me, but I managed to slip the strap off his shoulder in the process.

Instead of being able to pin me, he had to grab his sling shot.

I used that chance to pin his arms behind his back, then I flipped him over and wrapped my right arm around his thighs and pressed them back against his stomach, causing his shoulders to again touch the mat in a pin.

Before letting him go, I tugged on his loose sling shot and pulled it down around his thighs. This made it difficult for him to gain any freedom of movement and it exposed his genitals. His slender cock was rock hard and swollen almost purple. His nuts hung low between his legs, soft and fuzzy, full and round. I was tempted to give up the wrestling match and dive immediately into the middle of that delectable looking meal on a stick; but I knew that Gavin wanted to play the game all the way out to the finish.

I slid between his legs and pretended to butt fuck him, humping my hard cock against his exposed asshole, a tiny knot of pinkish-brown muscles surrounded by that same almost invisible blond fuzz of his. Still pushing his legs down against his chest, and admiring the fleshy scrotum which encased his sizeable nuts, I let my fucktool nudge his ass forcefully.

"I flipped you," I boasted; "so I guess that means I can dick you. Right?"

"Only if you can get your dick out of that jock strap without letting me up," he replied, pushing up with all his might, but unable to break the pin.

I leaned my body forward against the backs of his thighs, pressing real hard, to keep him bent in half while I quickly pulled my throbbing cock out of its elastic pouch.

I think he might have been expecting me to try to take the jock strap off completely, but I took him at his word and only pulled my cock out. It felt thick and swollen, pulsing and throbbing like a flesh wound, and so rock hard I couldn't have bent it with a pair of pipe wrenches. Then I rammed it up against his ass, poking several times to let him know I had succeeded. Without warning, I rammed real hard, penetrating the sphincter muscles.

He cried out, either in pain or in surprise. His ass was tight around my cock, but I pushed ahead and rammed it in as deep as I could get it, considering that his asshole had been dry except for the tiniest amount of sweat and that my cock had been dry except for a drop or two of pre-cum which eased out of the piss slit when I was poking him.

"Pull it out!" he cried. "Fuck! We gotta use Vaseline! That monster of yours will tear me apart."

The pleasure in the head of my dick was almost too intense to allow me the free will to pull out. With a mind of its own, it wanted to stay put. But I knew what it was like to have an unlubricated cock in my ass, and even though it can be pleasurable when done slowly and gently, I knew I had to have hurt him when I rammed it in; so I pulled out and eased up the pressure on his thighs, then I spread them apart and lay down on top of him.

"I suppose that means you want to get up and go find the Vaseline?" I asked, covering his mouth with a kiss before he could answer.

He wrapped his short, powerful legs around my torso and rubbed the heels of his feet against my sweaty buttocks. I was breathing hard and couldn't remember when I had so much fun having sex. Until now, sex had been routine—a pickup, an agreement as to who would do what to whom, a quickie, a few hot moments of passion, then an orgasm, followed by embarrassed good-byes. Gavin was more than twice my age, but sex was more pleasurable than it had ever been for me. Lying on top of him, after wrestling and playing with him, I realized how much fun sex could be. It didn't have to be *wham-bam thank-you ma'am.* Thinking all this, I kissed him even harder, sucking on his tongue and nibbling on his lips.

Before letting go, I squirmed around on top of his wet body, rubbing our cocks together and blending our sweat. He moaned with pleasure and I found myself moaning for the first time.

When I stopped kissing him, I rolled over on my right side, sliding off of him. I lay next to him, flat on the mat, breathing a little more slowly now.

He propped himself on his left elbow and began feeling my body with his right hand, gliding his fingers along my sweaty, slippery skin, feeling the hollow indentation of my stomach. At that age, I could suck my stomach in to a size twenty-seven inch waist.

At last, his fingers found my rigid piece of meat, jutting forward outside of the elastic jock pouch, begging for attention, and so hard that it bent back against my lower abdomen, forming a bridge from my nuts to my belly button across my hairless tummy (I mean, I didn't even grow a thin trail of hair on my stomach until

I was twenty).

He leaned over me and began to lick the sweat from my chest and nipples, then drew a path down to my cock with his tongue.

"I've changed my mind," he muttered softly. "I don't want you to fuck me, I want to suck you off. Right here and now."

I was in no mood to argue. His lips and tongue felt so good, so warm, so firm, so sensual that I wanted to just lie there and let him do his thing. My whole body was tingling with pleasure and I was ready to pop a nut with very little more coaxing. Gavin slipped his fingers into the waistband of the jock strap and pulled it off me, leaving me totally naked and feeling very much aware of my nudity. My body felt alive and shuddering with warm flashes from head to foot.

I watched him lick the tip of my dick with the point of his rigid tongue, then saw his moist lips close around the whole thickness of my shaft. He gently squeezed my nuts and I was afraid I would shoot my wad then and there. I wanted to hold off a little bit, for obvious reasons; so I tried to take my mind off what he was doing.

His body was bent in half, but he had swung his legs outward, away from me, in order to get into a more comfortable position. I let my hand glide along his back, which unlike the rest of him was completely free of that fine fuzz of blond hair. When my hand found his buns, I pulled on them, to indicate that I wanted him to come closer to me.

Following my hint, he brought the lower part of his body up toward my face and lay on his side, so I could get to his dick.

I rolled the upper part of my body to the right and propped myself on my right shoulder, slipping my right arm under his buns. His cock now loomed large before my eyes and I saw a drop of pre-cum glisten at the piss-slit. I licked it off and tasted the saltiness of his bodily juices. It danced up and down at the touch of my tongue and I experienced a powerful desire to wrap my lips around it and feel its hardness on my tongue.

He shuddered with delight and scooted even closer to my face. Now his cock was in my mouth and my fingers were toying with his asshole, causing it to pucker in expectation.

He lifted his left leg, bent it at the knee, and planted his left foot on the mat. This way, I was able to move my fingers between his thighs and gently stroke his nutsack.

He took my mind away from what I was doing by sucking so firmly on my cock that the pleasure was almost undeniable. I had to relax my groin muscles to avoid erupting into his mouth.

But he wouldn't let me off so easily; he began applying even more suction and more pressure. He sucked hard while his mouth rode up on my throbbing shaft; then he glided back down the length of my aching fuckmeat to its base, where his tongue dug into the underside of my pole. His fingers were busy scratching my balls and the insides of my thighs.

I tried doing the same thing to his cock, and suddenly I felt the surge of jism building in my nuts and spurting into the sperm ducts. The sperm raced to the head of my dick, then exploded into Gavin's mouth, while my body jerked and twisted in uncontrollable pleasure.

I sucked like a baby calf on Gavin's dick while he milked the cum out of mine. My stomach jack-knifed and I almost lost hold of his dick until I could relax my stomach muscles again. I shot load after load of hot cum into Gavin's mouth, until I thought my nuts would shrivel up from exhaustion, but Gavin continued to suck as if he never wanted me to quit shooting jizz into his throat.

My body thrashed and squirmed with intense feelings and I wrapped my legs around him and squeezed. I humped and pumped, and tried to fuck his face like a sex-starved maniac. I guess the excitement got to him, because I suddenly felt a squirting sensation along the length of his tubesteak. Then I tasted his salty juices again and I sucked on his cock the way he had done with mine.

My left arm was wrapped around his body and my left hand was feeling the silky fleshiness of his sides and hips, sliding around to the baby softness of his buns. His thick, swollen pole continued to jerk and squirt, emptying his hot cream onto my tongue. I squeezed his nuts, gently at first, then without thinking I found myself squeezing them too hard. I squeezed so hard he had to make me stop, but by then he had emptied their contents into my mouth and I had let the thick white liquid roll around on my tongue.

For a long time afterward, we continued to suck on each other's piece of meat. I started getting hard again, without actually going soft and Gavin resumed his suction, apparently in hopes of

KENNY AND HIS SURROGATE FATHER 73

bringing me to a second orgasm. I had to tell him that I could definitely cum again, but the second time always took me more than an hour, unless I managed to get a break in between.

He told me that he was pretty much the same way; he could cum five or six times a day, but he had to take a break in the action to recuperate. We agreed to pick up where we left off a little later. Earlier, right after he picked me up and offered to pay me a hundred bucks for spending the night, I had agreed to do it with him as often as he wanted. So now, not only was he paying for it, I was looking forward to it. He said he definitely wanted me to fuck him before the night was over, and he admitted that he was hot to shove his cock as far up my ass as he could drive it.

We took another bath in the Jacuzzi tub and talked while we let the relaxing waters play over our spent bodies. Gavin asked me if I was having a good time, and I said "Definitely."

We sat across from each other in the tub, and Gavin constantly played with my cock with his toes. Always following his lead, I placed my right foot in his crotch and wiggled my toes around, trying to excite him.

"Have you given any thought to going back home, Kenny?" he asked in a serious tone of voice.

"Never," I answered without hesitation. "I'll never go back. I'll miss my mom, but my dad can go take a flying fuck!"

"What are you going to do?"

I shrugged. "Who knows? I've managed to survive so far; I guess I'll keep on hustling until I get too old for it or can't find anyone willing to pay me for it."

"How much would you charge me to spend a whole week with me?" he asked. "Same conditions—sex whenever I want it. All you can eat and drink and all the sex you can handle."

I thought about it for a few minutes before answering. If I were to charge him a hundred bucks a night, then I should get seven hundred bucks a week. Right? Well, close to it.

"Before you answer," he interjected, "let me make you an offer. Three hundred dollars a week, plus room and board, and I'll even take you shopping and spend a couple of hundred bucks on clothes for you. Before you answer, let me tell you why I'm making this offer. Number one, I like you and I think you're one hell of a sexy young jock. I could have sex with you twenty-four hours a day and still want more." His toes played with my nutsack.

"Secondly, and more importantly, is this: if it works out and we like each other well enough to stick it out, I'm willing to let you move in and become my full-time lover. In addition to everything else, we'll enroll you in school when it starts and you can finish your high school education. You can live here, and tell everyone you're my nephew or something. You can have your own bedroom; I'll pay all of your expenses, plus give you a couple hundred dollars a week—like an allowance. You can't drive my Corvette, but if things work out, I'll buy you a sporty used car in a month or so."

I was having a hard time believing what I was hearing. I had been dreading having to leave the next morning, wondering where I would go or what I would do; and now he was offering me the whole world on a silver platter. I was stunned.

"There would be a lot of little things we'd have to work out, like house rules and so on; but I won't be like your father—I'll be like your lover. No one needs to know. I mean, for instance, at school, no one needs to know we have sex. To your classmates, I'm just your uncle. We'll work out a cover story. What do you say? You don't have much to lose, and as I see it, you've got everything to gain."

"Hell, yes!" I said enthusiastically. I surged across the tub and into his arms, splashing water all over the marble decking. "That's terrific!" He put up with my boyish antics for a couple of minutes, then made me sit back down. "We'll have to work out the details, but if we get past the first week, things should fall into place. We'll try it for a week, okay?"

I slumped down into the warm water, feeling better than I had ever felt in my life. This guy Gavin was just too great for words. I wouldn't have to go back to the streets to hustle for a living. Gavin would even buy me a car, when I got settled down in school. I couldn't believe it.

In the silence that followed, he picked up my right foot with both of his hands and pulled it closely to his mouth. He sucked on my toes with as much enthusiasm as he had sucked on my dick earlier.

I picked up his right foot and began sucking on his toes, too. It was almost as if we were sealing our agreement.

Later that night, we fucked. Even later, we sucked again and even fucked again. We couldn't seem to get enough sex with each other. The next morning, we slept till noon, went swimming in the nude, sucked each other off on the pool deck, and spent the whole day draining our testicles as soon as they had regenerated even a little bit of sperm.

As it turned out, I stayed with Gavin through high school and even started college. We had our share of arguments and fights, good times and bad; but for the most part, times were good. I left him when he found another young jock to take under his wings. We parted on good terms, though, because we understood each other, and we understood each other's needs.

I just wish all runaway street kids could have been as lucky as I had been.

CASEY AND
HIS LATCH-KEY FRIEND

The phrase "latch-key kids" came into prominence during the 1980's when it was discovered that more and more kids were being left alone after school because of working parents who couldn't be there to look after them. For most kids, it simply meant being able to have a little time to themselves without excessively close supervision. For others, the latch key opened the door to opportunities which might not have otherwise presented themselves. Casey was not, himself, a latch-key kid; his best friend was; but I'll let Casey tell you all about it. Casey is a good-looking kid with blue eyes and straw blond hair, which he always wears in the latest haircut styles; sometimes it's long, other times it's short, or even in-between. I met him when he was in his twenties; but in his teens, I'm sure he was just as sexy. His body has a natural firmness to it, unmarred by excessive bulk. He has hair on his chest, now, but not a lot; so I'm sure the teenager was as smooth as they come.

I GREW UP in a middle class home, in a middle class neighborhood, and went to a middle class high school. There was nothing remarkable or unusual about my childhood, except that I discovered I was gay just after reaching puberty. When everyone else in middle school was interested in girls, I couldn't help but think about boys.

My best friend, Dennis, turned out to be gay, too, and we found out that we could do a lot of things together that most other guys couldn't—especially have sex. Most poor bastards in middle school and high school can only beat their meat and make up lies about the girls they supposedly fucked. Me and Dennis didn't have to lie about having sex—we got all the sex we wanted. We didn't advertise the fact that we were sucking and fucking each other, but at the same time, we really didn't care who knew that we were gay.

We felt good about ourselves because we were able to release our pent-up sexual frustrations. Actually, that's all a bunch of bullshit—I mean it sounds like something I've read somewhere. The truth of the matter is: we didn't have *any* sexual frustrations; nothing got pent-up, because we usually got as much sex as we wanted. There was a lot of sexy guys in school that we looked at and talked about, and it would have been nice to have had sex with a lot of them; but you can't have everything, or *everyone* you want. We managed to coax some of them into bed with us, but most of the time, we just did each other, and said fuck the rest of the world.

We were lucky, because both of his folks worked and he didn't have any brothers or sisters to get in our way. His house was always empty after school. His folks never got home before six-thirty at night. During the summer, we had the house to ourselves all day long. If Dennis hadn't been a latch-key kid, we probably wouldn't have found out that each other was gay, because we might never have had the chance to play alone together.

We were twelve the first time we got naked together and started messing around. After that, it was a regular thing with us. And like I said, we sometimes brought other kids over to his house and fucked around.

During the summer vacation right after graduation from high school, Dennis hit on an idea that made us lots of money. He got the idea from that Tom Cruise movie, *Risky Business*, and figured what the Hell! He guessed we could probably make money as male prostitutes. He didn't go to the same extremes that Tom Cruise did. I mean, there were no thousand dollar weekends, or nothing like that, and it was harder finding customers, but between the two of us, we earned enough money to buy dirt bikes and Nintendos. The only thing our folks knew was that we worked every day of the week, doing odd jobs, and we saved our money. We always came up with good stories.

I don't know exactly where Dennis found his first customer, but the day it happened was a Tuesday. School had been out for a couple of weeks, and I went over to his house, as usual. His folks were at work, as usual. And Dennis was wearing nothing but cut-off jeans (with no underwear), as usual. I liked the way the cut-offs hung low on his narrow hips. He had a flat tummy and slender legs. If his buns hadn't been so round and beefy, those cut-offs would never have stayed up without a belt.

He was even skinnier when I first met him, but in high school he started to fill out. Although he was never muscular, he started putting some meat on his chest and on his buns. The strange thing was that whenever you saw him in his cut-offs, you felt like you were looking at him naked. I mean, they hung so low you thought you could see the top of his cock through the thin patch of pubic hair at the bottom of his long, narrow flat stomach, and there was no "pleasure trail" of hair starting at his belly button. His stomach was silky smooth. You saw so much of his flesh, you just felt like he was totally naked. I couldn't help myself, I always got horny just looking at him.

Whenever I went over to his house, I never wore underwear and I usually wore shirts that buttoned up the front, instead of pull-overs, which I didn't like because they always fucked up my hair when I took them off, which I almost always did when I went to see Dennis. That particular Tuesday, I was wearing a brightly colored polyester shirt, a pair of tennis shorts, which Dennis liked because they showed off my buns and the bulge of my dick in front, if I wasn't wearing a jock or any underwear (which I never did). They fit snugly against my thighs, and if I got even just a little bit hard, you could see the head of my cock through the material. If I got real hard, it strained against my leg and looked twice as big as it really is.

As much as we liked sex, we also liked looking and feeling sexy. We could never understand those straight guys who like to wear baggy shorts down to their knees, boxer undershorts, T-shirts, and three layers of clothing to hide their bodies. No wonder these guys never really scored with girls; they always looked like sex-less idiots out of some comic book. When a guy wears that much clothing, he just can't look sexy.

Dennis' house was on a corner lot, and I always jumped the fence and went to the back door. That morning, he was waiting for me by the pool and I could tell he was excited about something, because he was pacing back and forth. I wasn't late, or anything, but he acted like it.

He told me we were going to have sex that morning with a guy in his late twenties. The only thing unusual about that was the guy's age. Dennis usually found guys our same age, but I told him it might be kind of neat to do it with an older guy.

He told me the guy's name was Mike and that he was going to pay us to have sex with him. Dennis said that if it worked out, we might go into the sex-for-money business, like Tom Cruise in the movie. I said, okay, as long as we didn't have to do anything weird or kinky.

Dennis made me put on one of his skimpiest Speedos. It was a salmon color, which made me look almost naked. He put on a white one, then told me to get in the pool. When Mike showed up, I was supposed to get out of the water and just make sure that Mike got a good look at my body.

Dennis had made all the arrangements, and Mike showed up at the right time. He parked his car on the side street, then came to the side yard gate, which Dennis left open. When he came into the yard, I lifted myself out of the pool, dripping wet, and I couldn't help but notice how this guy Mike looked at my body, as if he wanted to lick me all over from head to toe.

"Do you want to go skinny dipping?" Dennis asked.

Mike looked nervous. "Maybe we'd better go inside."

Dennis led the way into the house, through the sliding glass door. Mike followed him and, after toweling off, I brought up the rear, carrying my tennis shorts.

The family room was pretty big, with a large screen TV, a couch, a couple of recliner chairs, a coffee table, and so on. Mike was nervous, but Dennis assured him that everything was cool. No one would come home unexpectedly. And even if they did, he'd hear the car in the driveway and there'd be plenty of time to ditch out the back door.

All three of us were nervous at first, but Dennis and I had worked as a team before, where we managed to get some guy out of his pants, even when he didn't suspect anything. In those cases, the guys were our own age; but we figured it would be easier with Mike, because Mike was expecting it.

Dennis walked up to him and started undoing his shirt buttons. Mike was taller and skinnier than either one of us, and he was sort of plain looking and hard to describe. His body was tightly muscular, with curly reddish-brown hair all over. The veins stood out in his arms, and his stomach had a wash-board effect. He was lanky, but you could tell his muscles were strong and powerful.

While Dennis removed Mike's shirt, I bent down between them and untied his shoe laces, then pulled his shoes and socks off. As soon as I moved away from them, Dennis went to work on Mike's jeans. In less than a minute, Mike was naked and his cock was already hard. I have to admit that it was one of the biggest cocks I'd ever seen. It was long and thick, the way mine looks through my tennis shorts when it's hard.

Dennis kissed Mike on the lips and they rubbed their bodies close together, while I took off my Speedos and came up behind Dennis. While those two were kissing and rubbing, I pulled Dennis' bathing suit off of him, slipping it down his legs to the floor. His firm, round buns looked so smooth and hairless and so big compared to his slender waist. I pressed myself against his back, shoved my dick between his legs, and wrapped my arms around him, reaching past him to feel Mike's hairy buns. I enjoyed the feel of my naked flesh against his. His body felt so hot and the heat transferred itself straight to the head of my cock, which I pumped back and forth between Dennis' ass cheeks.

After a few moments, Dennis slipped out from between us and took Mike by the hand and led him through the kitchen to the hallway. I followed them to Dennis' bedroom, where we'd had sex together more times than we could count, and sometimes with a third party.

It was a typical teenager's room, with posters and all sorts of paraphernalia on the wall and with nothing put away. There were clothes, books, games, and toys all over the floor and the bed was unmade.

Some people wouldn't like such a messy room, but for me and Dennis, this was the most comfortable place in the world. I'd be willing to bet that his rumpled bed sheets have seen more sex activity than the sheets of a lot of married couples. It seemed like we were always horny and always doing it, alone, together, or with someone else.

That bedroom just seemed like the best place in the world to have our threeway with Mike.

Like he used to do when we were younger, Dennis took a flying leap onto his mattress, face down. He bounced, rolled, and bounced again face up, spread eagle, his hard, swollen cock sticking straight up from the junction of his legs and pelvis like a tent stake sticking out of the ground.

I was right behind Mike, who stopped just inside the room, blocking my way. He was looking at Dennis' naked body spread out on the bed, invitingly seductive and sexy as hell. I placed my hands on Mike's hairy buns and nudged him forward. At the foot of the bed, he crawled between Dennis' slender, hairless legs and lowered himself onto Dennis' lean body, into his waiting arms. I crawled on top of Mike, sandwiching him between me and Dennis. The mattress was plenty soft and, although Dennis was squashed down pretty deep, I knew that Mike and I weren't hurting him.

I pushed my cock between Mike's thighs, near his buns, and I began to hump him, even though my dick just barely touched his ass. My humping caused Mike to hump on Dennis and the whole bed got to bouncing as if we were on a trampoline. Dennis and I both knew that his bed could take all sorts of pounding and abuse; a simple little threeway action was nothing for that old warrior!

There were three sets of naked legs on the bed, wrestling and intertwined with each other in the sheets and coverlet. One set of legs was as hairy as a wolf and the other two sets were smooth and hairless. Our swollen cocks throbbed with lust and hot passion; each one of them was anxious to find a hot, moist hole to climb into and work itself into a frenzy. Our three assholes were twitching with expectation.

Being on the bottom of that heap of hot, naked flesh, however, was confining and restrictive; so Dennis groaned, letting us know that he wanted out. I rolled off to his left side and let Mike roll off to his right side. All three of us were lying face up on the bed.

As it happened, Dennis' hands fell on top of both our crotches, as he struggled to regain his breath, and he grabbed our dicks as if they were handlebar safety grips. I rolled over on my side and looked at his hot, nude body, panting and writhing with pleasure. I ran my hand down his fleshy chest and stomach and teased his balls, then felt his dick. I suppose I should have tried to show more interest in Mike, but even though the guy was hot and sexy, I still preferred sex with Dennis, and I like his body better than anyone else's.

Mike wasn't being left out, though. Dennis was making sure the guy was getting his money's worth. And I think Mike was like me, in that he also preferred Dennis' body. After catching his breath, Mike leaned over and down and sucked Dennis' cock into his mouth. He was bent at his waist, with his right leg up, bent at the knee. I scooted down the bed and leaned over Dennis' thighs and came up between Mike's legs and spread them apart in order to get at his pulsating shaft. His cock was thick and long, with veins that stood out like the ones in his biceps and forearms. His helmet was spongy and shiny, plump like the rubber ball used in a game of jacks.

We took turns sucking each other, stroking each other, feeling each other, and just generally doing whatever felt good for the next fifteen or twenty minutes. At the end of that time, we were ready to bust our nuts, but none of us really wanted to bring it to an end.

After awhile, we worked ourselves into this position: Mike was sitting on the edge of the bed with Dennis sitting in his lap, facing me. I was on the floor kneeling in front of Dennis, with my mouth wrapped around his cock. With my left hand, I was feeling their legs and mentally making note of the sharp contrast between them. With my right hand, I was feeling their balls; both scrotums were soft and fuzzy. Dennis' hung low enough to almost touch Mike's. Mike's fuck rod was jammed up Dennis' ass and the guy was bouncing up and down on the bed, his hands feverishly feeling Dennis' body everywhere his fingers could reach.

Dennis has always liked having a thick cock up his ass, and this time he was getting it good! In addition to Mike's swollen piece of meat being shoved up his ass, Dennis had my mouth wrapped around his cock, sucking him and milking him toward a climax. By this time, Dennis couldn't hold back any longer and I felt his cock expand and contract as he squirted hot cum into my mouth. His jerking motions let Mike know that he'd shot his load; so Mike started bouncing even faster, driving himself to an orgasm.

As soon as I had sucked all of Dennis' sweet tasting cum out of his reddish-pink fuck tube, I stood up and shoved my cock into his face. He had to bend a little to get it into his mouth, and even then it wasn't easy, because Mike was bouncing the bed so furiously; but as soon as he managed to line up his mouth with my dick, he vacuumed it in so fast, I thought he would make me cum in an instant. The feel was electric and drove me wild with sexual sensations that made my dick tingle. I was just about ready to shoot my wad and wouldn't be able to hold off much longer.

I think Mike and me hit our climaxes right at the same time. Poor Dennis had me slamming my dick into his face and Mike pounding his dick up his ass. Mike was holding onto Dennis' pectoral muscles so tightly that there were light bruise marks afterward, and I had dug my fingers into Mike's shoulders, holding onto him for balance while jacking my cock into Dennis' mouth with the relentless pounding of a trip hammer. Dennis was holding onto my buns and was trying to slip one of his fingers into my puckering asshole. He managed to insert one of his fingers past my sphincter muscles just as I was ramming my cock home inside his mouth, gushing hot cum into his throat.

The three of us sort of collapsed all at once. It had worked out great. Dennis had reached his orgasm before me and Mike, but not by much, and it allowed me to get my rocks off before the party was over. Mike had definitely gotten what he had paid for. He told Dennis that he'd like to do it again sometime soon.

After Mike was gone, Dennis showed me the two fifty dollar bills he had gotten from Mike. I hadn't seen the money change hands, but Dennis told me it happened while I was toweling off before coming inside.

He then told me that there was lots more where that came from. Dennis had learned from this other guy he knew that there was a place downtown where guys hung out waiting to get picked up by men who were willing to pay to have sex with them. Most of the time, the sex took place in a car; but Dennis had decided that he and I could do a lot better than that. We not only offered three-ways, we had a house and a bed to do it in.

As the summer wore on, Dennis took me to the "meat rack," as everyone called it, more and more often, and I helped him drum up business for our three-ways. Most of the kids at the "meat rack" did their business at night; me and Dennis did ours during the day and it was amazing how many customers we picked up. Not every one wanted to have a three-way; so sometimes, we did it one-on-one.

We never did get caught, because Dennis' parents never came

home during the day (except on Sundays). And we made a hell of a lot of money. Like I said, we even bought dirt bikes that summer.

We kept it up when we started college, but after awhile, it became too much work and we slowed down considerably. It was great while it lasted, but I don't think they'll ever make a movie about it. Especially not with Tom Cruise.

LAREN AND THE GUY WHO BOUGHT HIS SHORTS

Reddish brown hair, brown eyes, freckles, and pale white skin. That's the only fair description of Laren, who is as Irish as they come. What makes him attractive is the shape of his nose, the angle of his jaw, and the way his lips form a pout when he's not smiling. Without any clothes on, he looks like a little boy; that is to say, his small frame never filled out with noticeable muscular development. His nipples are incredibly flat and pale and look like nothing more than two large freckles on his highly freckled body. He's not so skinny that his ribs show, but his stomach is flat enough to form a hollow between his hips. His legs are slender and hairless, and his feet look a little bit too large for his body. His uncut cock is average in length and thickness, but it hangs nicely plump in the flaccid state, and is framed by a thin patch of strawberry blond pubic hair, which takes on a reddish-pink tint against his white skin. If you like redheads, Laren would be your dream come true. It's easy to overlook him in a crowd, because unless he's the center of attraction, he blends into the background; but when you talk with him, his impish, puckish personality wins you over instantly.

I KNEW I was gay when I was eight years old. I kept trying to seduce my Uncle Mike, whenever he came over to use our pool. He didn't like little boys (sexually speaking, that is), and at first he thought I was just being playful with him; but after awhile, he could see I was serious. When he told my folks that his nephew was going to grow up to be a fag, he and my dad had a big fight. For years they wouldn't talk to each other, and Uncle Mike stopped coming over to our house.

Dad didn't want to believe Uncle Mike, but the idea that his son might grow up to be a "queer" scared him just enough that he started taking steps to see to it that I grew up "straight." If I did anything at all that my dad thought was girlish or unmanly, he would beat me with his razor strop. I wanted to take up the clarinet and join the school band, but he wouldn't let me have anything to do with music (especially a *long, tubular* instrument like the clarinet). I wanted to try out for the school play one year, but he wouldn't let me do that, either. He wouldn't let me do anything I wanted to do. He demanded that I get active in sports, as if that makes every boy a man!

For me, getting into sports was okay, because even though I was never very good at anything, I got to shower with the other boys and got to see them naked. None of the coaches ever let me play, because I was just too awkward and too uncoordinated. But, as far as my dad was concerned, the only important thing was that I was "trying," even if I never did anything more than warm the bench. At least I wasn't being a "sissy"; at least I wasn't prancing around on a stage. At least I wasn't sucking on a long black tube.

My best friend in school was a handsome kid named Edwin. I met him in the tenth grade, when we were both taking swimming. He was real good looking and very well built. He was also gay, and after we became best friends, we used to fuck around a lot, sexually. Every chance we got, we had sex. We taught each other everything we ever learned about sex: how to suck, how to fuck, how to make each other feel good, how to sixty-nine, and so on.

My dad's best intentions to make sure I didn't grow up and become a faggot got all fucked up when Edwin and I became best friends, but my dad didn't know it. He thought Edwin was straight, because he behaved so butch and was active in all kinds of sports. I laughed every time I thought how pleased my dad was that I had such a jock like Edwin for a friend.

It surprised the hell out of him when he caught Edwin fucking me in the ass one day after school. He came home early and found me and Edwin on the living room carpet. My white little butt was beat until it turned black and blue, and he didn't stop there. My back and my legs were also beaten so severely that I developed welts and horrible bruises all over. It's no exaggeration to say that I couldn't hardly walk for a week.

My dad told Edwin's dad all about the way he caught us, butt naked and fucking each other like two fairies. Edwin's father made life miserable for him, and Edwin ran away from home a few days later. He came and got me and we ran away together, even though I was so sore it was hard to move.

When all this happened, we were both seventeen and we didn't think our folks would call the cops on us; but they did. We got busted a couple days later and they threw our asses in Juvenile Hall. Our parents asked the courts to declare us "incorrigible" and so we ended up staying in Juvie until we turned eighteen.

Edwin was two months older than me; so he got out first. He knew what day my birthday fell on and he promised to be there on the day I got out.

Those two months without him were miserable. Juvie really bites it big time. I mean, it sucks! You've got little kids trying to be big shots; you've got big kids trying to boss the little kids; you've got wimps trying to prove how strong they are; and you've got tough guys who talk bad about faggots, but then go around trying to rape the little guys. You've got counselors who think their shit don't stink. You've got bad food, and stupid rules, and assholes everywhere.

After Edwin left, there was just one kid I made friends with. Him and me, we sucked each other's dick whenever we could find a place to be alone. It was hard to find a place comfortable enough to fuck each other and not get caught.

On my eighteenth birthday, they cut me loose. Edwin proved he really was my best friend by being there, waiting for me across the street. My dad was there, too, trying to hassle me and give me a bad time. I just told him to go fuck himself in the ass and me and Edwin turned our backs on him and walked away.

In the two months since he got out, Edwin had picked up a new trade. Street hustling. He told me all about it. I was surprised as hell when he told me how much money he made at it, and he wanted me to give it a try. I liked having sex with Edwin, and with guys my own age, but I wasn't sure I could warm up to the idea of having sex with a stranger.

He told me I had a choice: I could either put on a paper cap and work my butt off at a fast food restaurant for minimum wage, or I could really use my butt and make fifty to a hundred bucks a night, maybe even more, depending on how hard I wanted to work and how many tricks I wanted to turn. The only thing involved was having sex—sucking and fucking. Sex was fun, right? What did I want to do? Serve french fries and cokes? Or have sex and make a lot of money doing what I like to do best?

He made it sound real simple and told me that he had the perfect customer in mind for me for my first trick. I told him, I'd try it. But if I didn't like doing it, I was going to quit.

Edwin told me he had saved up a lot of cash and it surprised the hell out of me when he showed me a roll of bills and said it was over seven hundred dollars—and that was after living expenses. He bought me some nice clothes and took me to lunch, then we went to this room he was renting by the week in a motel. Later, we ordered pizza, then he told me to put on the new clothes he had bought for me.

"Tonight you've got to wear underwear, but usually it's best if you don't. The first time I went to this guy's house, where we're going tonight, I wasn't wearing any underwear, and he told me to come back when I had some on." He didn't explain what he meant, and I didn't think to ask.

That night, he took me to a large condominium apartment complex in the nicer part of town. A guy in one of the upper apartments buzzed us in and we rode the elevator to his floor. There was no one in the hallway, and the guy's door was open, so we just went right on in.

The apartment was super modern, with plush carpeting and heavy furniture. The living room windows overlooked the city and at night the lights were really fantastic.

Edwin introduced me to Howard and told me he was a lawyer. Howard couldn't take his eyes off me. I mean, seriously, this guy was undressing me with his eyes. I've got to admit that I never thought I was good looking, or anything, but this guy looked at me like I was some kind of teen idol. He invited us into his huge living room and offered us mixed drinks.

Howard was in his forties, or maybe his early fifties; it was hard to tell, because he was very distinguished looking. He had dark brown hair, with gray at the temples and his face sort of reminded me of Paul Newman. When he handed us our drinks, he said to Edwin, "I like your friend. I've always had this thing for redheads."

Then he said to me, "You're a very stunning young man. Has

Edwin told you what I like?"

I thought about it for a second, and realized that, no, he hadn't told me anything at all. "No," I answered. "I'm new at this."

"Even better," Howard said. "I don't usually have more than one boy up here at a time, but in your cases, I'll make an exception. We'll let Edwin handle all the details."

Edwin told me to just do what he did, and we sat there and drank our drinks, talking for awhile. Then Edwin reached down and untied his shoes, took them off, and removed his socks. I waited till he was finished, then I did the same thing. The carpet felt plush and thick against my bare toes.

Howard was wearing dress slacks and a silk shirt, open in front all the way down. His feet were bare. It was obvious to me that it wouldn't take him long to get naked.

Edwin and I were sitting on an overstuffed couch near the center of the room. Howard was sitting in a chair across from us, separated by a brass coffee table with a glass top. There wasn't a lot of furniture, considering the huge size of the room; but I guess that's what made it look so big.

Edwin asked if he could fix another drink and Howard said it was okay. He stood up and took off the brand new shirt he had bought for himself that afternoon when he was buying clothes for me; he tossed it over the back of a chair that wasn't being used; then he went to the bar, which was near the end of the wall that joined the outside wall at a right angle. I wondered if people could see inside the apartment on a night like this. Would they be able to see us if we got completely naked? Probably not, but it made me nervous thinking about it.

I stood up and took my shirt off and threw it on the back of the same chair. When I turned to reach for my drink, Howard startled me. He had come around the coffee table and had picked up my cocktail glass. He now stood right next to me, smiling at me, handing me my drink.

I took the glass from him and his hands immediately reached toward my new Dockers slacks. "Let me help you with those," he said as he started undoing the buttons.

Edwin came back with his drink, set it down, and took my glass from me. "I'll fix you one, too," he said. "You and Howard have fun."

Before I knew it, Howard had me out of my pants and was kneeling in front of me with his mouth on my shorts, blowing hot air on my cock through the cotton material. In spite of myself, I couldn't help but start to get a hardon. I felt my prick stiffening, and I felt his hot breath and the pressure of his lips. He braced himself by holding onto my buns. I felt awkward as hell, because I hadn't ever done something like that for money and I didn't know what to do; but his hot air and his lips made me feel really good.

He brought his right hand around and slipped a couple fingers into my shorts, near my balls. At first, I felt ticklish and I was afraid I was going to laugh; but he lightly scratched my nuts with a finger nail, and instead of being ticklish, it was sexy as hell.

Edwin came up behind me, handed me my drink, then snuggled his crotch into my back. I felt his hard cock through his pants. Then I felt Howard's left hand starting to undo Edwin's pants. As soon as they were unbuttoned, Edwin stepped back and took them off.

He then walked around us and stood behind Howard. He took the guy's shirt off while he was still blowing hot air on my dick through my shorts. By now, my cock was raging hard and fully erect. Howard had no difficulty wrapping his mouth all around it, even through the cotton, and his fingers were going to town on my balls, teasing them and tickling them lightly, except for when Edwin removed his right shirt sleeve.

I wondered how soon we would all get naked; but just as I was wondering, Edwin caught my attention and did a little pantomime. He stood back from Howard, shoved his hands into the waistband of his shorts, then shoved them downward, but during this he was shaking his head, "No." He pushed his shorts so low, he exposed the top part of his cock. He's got a beautiful cock. It's thick, and long, and circumcised.

Next, Edwin pulled his shorts back up, then reached in and pulled out his tool. He slipped the waistband of his shorts down under his nuts, showing me that it was okay to pull my dick out, but not okay to take off my underwear.

Edwin's body was magnificent. He was always good at sports and he had developed a pretty good build. Just looking at him would have given me a hardon, even if Howard hadn't been giving me a blow job.

Anyway, I got the idea that Edwin was trying to tell me: don't take off your shorts; when you pull your dick out, leave your shorts on.

Howard stood up and we drank our drinks, then we sat down on the couch, with Howard between me and Edwin. He put his hands inside our shorts and felt our cocks, stroking us to make sure we were good and hard.

While he was doing that, Edwin undid Howard's belt, then undid the buttons on his slacks. With Howard's help, and with mine, Edwin got his pants all the way down. Howard pulled his hands out of our shorts and took his pants the rest of the way off. Then he slid down off the couch and rolled over in front of Edwin, on his knees, with his head buried in Edwin's lap. He did the same thing to Edwin he had been doing to me: he sucked on his cock through his shorts.

Watching Howard do Edwin like that made me horny as hell, and I stuck my hand into my shorts and started stroking my cock. I wanted to be where Howard was. The only difference was, I didn't want to suck on Edwin's shorts, I wanted to suck on the real thing. I wanted the solid flesh of his naked cock in my mouth.

Edwin reached way over and pulled my shorts away from my cock, letting me know that if I was going to jack off, I was supposed to pull it out and do it out in the open.

I've never been circumcised, and even when I'm hard, the foreskin completely covers the head of my dick unless I pull it back. It's neat, because whenever I jack off, I can literally trap the sperm in the folds of my foreskin, so that it doesn't get all over everything. Then I can take some tissue paper and soak up all that hot cum, then wipe off the head of my dick. I never have to worry about getting cum all over my hands or in my shorts or in the sheets, or whatever. When I was living at home, I never had to worry about my mom finding cum stained sheets. On the other hand, I can pull the foreskin back and let it fly, if I want. Edwin and I used to do that once in a while, just to see who could shoot the farthest. This ability to control my own jizz is the only neat thing about being uncut. I think a circumcised cock looks nicer than one that isn't.

Well, anyway, I pulled my shorts down under my nuts, then

began to stroke my cock, pulling the foreskin back and forth over the head of my dick. Howard looked over at me and immediately let go of Edwin's cock.

"Ah, you're uncut!" he exclaimed, as if it was the greatest thing since sliced bread. He moved in front of me, still on his knees on the floor. He pushed my hand out of the way and took over for me, stroking my meat, moving the foreskin back and forth over the cap of my cock. "I love the way the head appears and disappears on an uncircumcised cock. And I love sticking my tongue into the foreskin."

He then proceeded to do just that. He pulled the skin back, exposing my shiny dickhead, pressed his tongue up against it, then pulled the foreskin forward over his tongue. I felt his tongue moving around beneath the skin over the sensitive head of my dick.

Edwin got up and straddled me on the couch. It's hard to explain how he did it, but while Howard was on the floor, sucking my cock and playing with my nuts, Edwin was on the couch with his cock in my face, his backside toward Howard.

I loved having Edwin's cock in my mouth. I was now so hot and excited that I knew I was going to cum pretty quick. I think Edwin knew it, too, because he said, "Be sure to let Howard know just before you're going to cum. He wants you to cum in your shorts, not in his mouth."

So, that was the reason for the shorts! It was starting to make sense.

After a moment of sucking on Edwin's thick, swollen cock, I nudged him away and said, "I'm going to cum!"

Howard took his mouth away and quickly pulled my shorts up to cover my dick. But as soon as he took his mouth away, I wasn't able to cum. I told him so, and he started jacking me off through the shorts. Edwin put his cock back in my mouth and then it didn't take very long at all. Howard stuck his fingers back into my shorts from the bottom and played with my nuts just as I shot my wad into the cotton material. I had to reach into the top of my shorts to pull the foreskin all the way back to let the cum shoot into the cotton material. Some of it got on my stomach, of course, but most of it was soaked up by the shorts.

While this was happening, I reached my left hand into the backside of Edwin's shorts and felt his round, smooth buns, then put my index finger into his asshole. He liked that, and he started pumping my face even faster.

But then, suddenly, he pulled out and rolled away from me. He gasped out loud: "I'm ready, Howard."

Howard moved from me to Edwin and sucked him off through his shorts. I leaned over and kissed Edwin on the lips while he was catching his nut.

All this time, Howard had never played with his own cock, nor had he ever taken it out. I wondered if he was impotent, or if he just had a kinky thing about getting boys to shoot their wads in their shorts while he watched and felt and touched. We never did find out; even Edwin didn't know the answer to that.

As soon as we were through shooting our hot cum into our underwear, Howard got up and fixed us another drink. When we finished with them, Edwin said it was time to go and Howard pulled out his wallet. He gave each of us a fifty dollar bill. I said thanks and started to put my Dockers on, but Edwin stopped me and said, "No, Laren. Howard is buying your shorts. You gotta take 'em off and give 'em to him. That's what the fifty bucks is for."

We both stripped out of our shorts and handed them to Howard, who put them to his nose and breathed deeply. He seemed to be pleased with what he had bought.

That night, back at Edwin's motel room, I told him that, since everything had gone so smoothly, I would probably take up street hustling. It hadn't been that bad, and the money was great. Edwin said that he had a lot to teach me, but he told me that I already knew the basics: how to suck and how to fuck. The rest would come with experience.

I've had thousands of tricks, since then, but Howard was the only one who ever wanted to buy my shorts.

RANDY AND
DOOR-TO-DOOR SALES

When you've finished reading Randy's story, you'll not be surprised to learn that he was in prison for Obtaining Money Under Fraudulent Pretenses. It was something he learned how to do early in life. However, I find I can't be too harsh on him, because from what I can tell, people get what they pay for and in Randy's case, the product and the services appear to be worth every penny of what a person might pay for them. Randy wasn't always as beefed-up as he is now, because he developed a lot of his bulk on the weight pile in prison; but I would be willing to bet that his body held the promise of future development while he was still in his teens. His hair is dark brown, his eyes are dark brown, and his complexion is dark bronze, except below his tan line, where the contrast between prison pallor and prison suntan is striking. He lays out in the sun every chance he can get, but he assures me that "on the streets" he doesn't allow a tan line to develop; he likes to sunbathe in the nude.

I've been on my own since I was thirteen. When I wasn't doing time in juvenile hall, I was hustling on the streets. I don't know who my real parents are, or even if they're still alive: I was adopted when I was a little kid. The people who adopted me were real sickos. They were the most hypocritical Bible-thumpers I've ever run across. I could tell you stories about those two freaks to make your hair stand on end. Everyone thought they were model citizens, but I knew better, and I've got a few scars to prove it. I moved out when I was thirteen, because they were just getting too kinky and too weird.

For several years, the only way I could support myself was by selling my body. It was fun and exciting at first, but after awhile, the excitement and adventure wore off. When it comes to hustling on street corners, you never knew who was going to pick you up or what they were going to want to do to you. I like sex and all that, but hustling for sex just wasn't the same as having sex for fun. I couldn't help but think of my "parents" every time I turned a trick. So for the most part, I tried to find other ways to make money. One time I answered an ad in the paper for high school kids to earn extra money. It was door to door magazine sales.

That was when I found out how easy it is to make money going from door to door. You can sell anything, if you've got the right pitch. You can also sell yourself, if you're good looking and if you've got a nice body. And it sure beats standing on a street corner. And people are less likely to be weird in their own house.

Magazine sales are a good gimmick for high school graduates making money for college. Everyone wants to help a clean-cut, good-looking guy make it into college, right? You'd be surprised how much! Men and women, both, would invite me in to talk about which magazines they would subscribe to. It's amazing how many of them will offer beer or even hard liquor to a teenager, just to loosen him up a little. Well, I can assure you, I loosened up a lot. I always made a minimum of fifty bucks a day, and that was on a slow day. I sold a lot of magazine subscriptions, too.

After awhile, I learned that houses were good for actually selling magazines, but they weren't really the best customers when it came to selling sex; apartment buildings turned out to be the most lucrative. Most residential areas are occupied by married couples and their children. The customers that turned the most money for me were singles, both male and female.

I'm definitely gay. I like men and men are what turn me on, sexually. But sex is sex, and even a gay teenager can fuck a hot babe. But usually, the babes who wanted to pay me for sex were middle aged or older. Come to think of it, so were most of the men.

When you spend all day long, and half the night, sucking and fucking for a living, sex starts to get a little stale, though. When this story happened, all I was doing was living from one day to the next, from one trick to the next. I was thinking about hitch hiking out to California (which I did, but I never got past Nevada, as it turns out).

I needed a little extra pocket money; so I decided to turn a few more tricks before hustling my ass out to the West Coast. I found an apartment building I hadn't worked before, but after lots of no answers, I decided to go back that night. In the meantime, I bought a new receipt book and decided to splurge on a new summer shirt, something light and airy, one which I could unbutton down the front to show off my tanned, smooth, hairless chest. At seven o'clock, I went back to the apartment building and quickly made several "sales," without even being invited in for a beer.

At one of the apartments, the door was answered by a really great looking blond guy in his early twenties. The weather was warm and he was wearing nothing but a pair of cut-off jeans. He was kind of thin, but he wasn't skinny. I mean, he was nicely muscular, without being muscle-bound. He looked the way I imagined all those California surfers would look, when I got there. He was drinking a beer and I guess he and his roommate had been laughing about something, because he had a big grin on his face when he opened the door.

I went into my magazine sales pitch, but I had a hard time taking my eyes off the bulge in his crotch, because the outline of his cock showed through the material of his cut-offs. This guy was a real fox and for the first time since I could remember, I was actually getting hot for one of my prospective customers. It was strange for me, because sex had become so boring that instead of looking forward to it, I had gotten to the point where I dreaded it.

He stopped me in the middle of my memorized spiel and invited me in. His roommate came out of the kitchen and, when he saw me, he handed me the beer he had just opened. The roommate was even better looking than the blond, but in a different way. He was like a college jock or something; by that I mean, he had an athlete's body and he looked like he played a lot of sports. His chest was big and muscular, and his biceps and forearms were powerfully built. He had brown hair and blue eyes and a creamy chocolate tan. He was wearing athletic shorts which showed off his muscular legs. They were both barefoot, and they looked like a couple of college kids, partying over the weekend.

The blond guy sat next to me on the couch in the living room and introduced himself. His name was Woody. His roommate's name was Alexander, but everyone just called him Sandy. They asked a lot of the typical questions of a kid who goes from door to door selling magazine subscriptions: Was I planning to go to college? How many subscriptions do I have to sell? How old am

I? Where am I from? What college do I plan to go to? And on and on.

I gave them my standard answers, lying through my teeth, of course. But I was enjoying talking to them because they were treating me like a younger brother and they really seemed to care about me getting into college. Before I knew it, they were handing me a second beer. We were talking a lot and getting to know each other. Woody was a Liberal Arts major and Sandy didn't know what he was going to settle on for a major; maybe engineering, he said. What about me? Business Management, I said.

Sandy started talking about college sports and wanted to know if I played anything special. When I told him that I wasn't athletically inclined, he said, "Bullshit! You look like you'd be good at sports. Stand up for a second."

When I stood up, he told me, "Take off your shirt. Let's see what you look like."

Until that moment, I thought that I was the only one there who was interested in having sex. But when Sandy wanted to look at my chest, it suddenly began to look more promising. I gladly took off my shirt and showed them my body. I'm not as well built as Sandy, and maybe not as tightly muscled as Woody, but I'm proud of what I've got.

Sandy took my shirt away from me and took it into the kitchen where he draped it over a chair. He obviously didn't want me to put it back on right away. In the meantime, Woody was feeling my biceps, telling me to "make a muscle." Then Sandy came back and said, "Let me feel your pecs."

Without waiting for my permission, he put his hands on my chest and felt my pectoral muscles, which aren't big, but they're not flat, either. My chest is just sort of naturally filled out. I've never had to work out with weights or anything to have what looks like a good build. Sandy complimented me on a fine body, but he didn't stop feeling me up. He even rubbed his finger tips over my nipples several times.

He was getting me all hot and bothered. I felt my cock starting to stiffen up. I was enjoying all the attention, but I wasn't used to having people come on to me so quickly. These guys were moving too fast for me. In the past, if some guy was going to try to put the make on me, he usually went a lot slower. A man has to be careful in case the guy like me turns out to be a fag-basher or something worse. But Woody and Sandy were all over me, feeling me up and talking about muscles and how perfect my body was for sports.

When Sandy said he wanted to check out my legs, I told him I wasn't wearing any underwear. I thought he would drop the subject, but instead, he bent down in front of me and felt my legs through my jeans. My hardon was getting bigger and I'm pretty sure he noticed it. While his hands were running up and down my thighs, he rubbed against my crotch several times.

Then he stood up in front of me, so close I could feel his hot breath on my face. He had a little smile on his face when he said, "Let's see how your thighs compare to mine or Woody's."

I felt a rush of hot sexual excitement sweep over my face. All I could say was, "I already told you, I'm not wearing any underwear."

"That's no problem," he said. "I'll let you wear my jock strap, if it'll make you feel better." He pulled off his shorts right in front of me and stood there with nothing on but a jock strap, which showed a sizeable hunk of meat stuffed into the rib knitting of the pouch. He flung his shorts into the hall, then pulled off the jock strap, allowing his thick piece of fuckflesh to dangle free. It wasn't hard, yet, but I could tell that it was getting thicker and it was starting to stick outward from his body. He held his jock strap out toward me and said, "Here. Put this on, if you're shy. Me and Woody don't get bashful in front of other guys."

As if to prove the point, Woody unbuttoned his cut-offs and let them fall to the floor. He wasn't wearing anything beneath them and his long slender cock grabbed my attention. "Come on," he said, "there's no one here but us guys. Let's see what you got."

Did he mean my legs? Or did he mean my cock? I wasn't ashamed of either one, but these guys were moving so fast, I was having a hard time keeping up. I've got to admit that I wanted to get naked with them, but I was also a little bit afraid. There was two of them, and I had a hardon. What if it turned out they weren't gay? What if they were just fucking with me? What if they were gonna get me naked, then throw me outside? It was unlikely as hell, but what if?

"I really should be going," I said, although I don't know why

I said it. "I've got a quota to meet. I've still got to sell fifty dollars worth of magazines, tonight." That was the line I usually used when I was setting my price for some guy who wanted to have sex with me. I don't know why I used it with these two guys, though. After all, I was the one who wanted to have sex. I felt like I was going to fuck this whole thing off. Why did I open my big mouth?

"Fifty bucks?" Woody said. "That's a lot of money. I don't think we can help you."

Sandy said quickly, "We can't help you with all of it, but we can probably come up with twenty bucks or so. Will that help?"

I was glad he said it, because it gave me the reprieve I needed. "Yeah, that'll help a lot."

"Well, then, forget about magazines for awhile. Let's get back to what we were talking about. Let's take a look at your thighs." He reached down and unbuttoned my jeans. My cock bounced out like a jack in the box when someone cranks the lid open. It was hard and thick, and there was no mistaking the fact that I was sexually aroused.

Sandy pushed my snug jeans down to my knees, then said, "Looks like we've all got the same idea." He wrapped his hand around my swollen cock and stroked it.

These guys had been moving pretty fast for me; but now they really turned on the speed. Woody disappeared down the hall, and I watched his firm round buns flex and relax with each step he took, pumping like the pistons in a car engine. I didn't know where he was going, but I didn't have time to think about it, because Sandy wrapped his arms around me and kissed me. Then he leaned me backward and we flopped onto the couch, still kissing each other. I felt his naked body rub against my chest and groin. Our cocks were touching and I felt a surge of hot excitement rush through my dickhead.

When Sandy pulled his mouth away from mine, I looked up and saw Woody with a large rubber sheet. He spread it out on the floor near the kitchen. It covered the carpet and overlapped into the kitchen by just a couple of inches.

Sandy began to lick my chest and stomach, ignoring Woody. It looked like he was going straight for my cock. He eased himself off the couch and slid between my legs, where my jeans were crumpled in a bunch around my knees. Just as he wrapped his lips around my cock, Woody came up behind him, knelt down, and took my shoes and socks off me. He leaned over Sandy, felt me up, looked at me with those large blue eyes of his, kissed me, then went into the kitchen.

Sandy then turned loose of my swollen prick and pulled the jeans away from my body. With clockwork precision, I had been stripped naked and the apartment had been converted into an orgy arena.

Sandy stood up, pulled me up by the arms, then led me to the rubber sheet. Woody poured about half a bottle of Wesson oil onto it, then lay down on it and began to writhe around in the oil. It was exciting as hell to watch his surfer body slither around in all that oil. It didn't take much coaxing for me to get down into it with him. Soon, the three of us were wallowing around in the oil, rubbing each other's body, smearing the oil around, slipping and sliding against each other.

It was then that I noticed that Woody shaved the pubic hairs around his cock and balls, leaving only a small triangular patch of hair above his penis. I discovered that he shaved his legs, too. (Actually, when I talked to him about it later, he told me he used *Neet* hair remover—it left him feeling silky as hell and it had a nice coconut aroma.) He didn't remove the hair from his arms or from his armpits, because he thought it might be too noticeable in public, and he didn't need to use it on his chest, because he didn't have any chest hair. I was amazed at how soft and smooth his body felt. The combination of the hair remover and salad oil made him so slippery and so slimy smooth, it was unreal.

Sandy felt slippery, too, but he just wasn't as slick as Woody. Sandy's hair wasn't coarse or wiry, but compared to Woody's smooth, hairless body, Sandy's skin seemed rough and fuzzy. I enjoyed the contrasts between the feelings of each of their bodies, even though it's hard to describe. I loved the different sensations I got from each one of them. They were so different from each other, so perfect together. One had blue eyes with blond hair, and was smooth as hell; the other had brown hair, blue eyes, and a muscular body with a soft coat of light hair. One was slender; one was beefy. I was sort of in between.

And when I say I was in between, I mean it in more ways than one. Before long, I was between Sandy and Woody in a sandwich; but a sandwich on a rubber sheet covered with salad oil is a tricky proposition. There's just no way to gain any traction. At one point, my cock was positioned right at Woody's ass, but when I tried to shove it in, my knees just slid out from under me. It would have been funny or comical, if we hadn't been so fucking hot and bothered. The three of us just couldn't get enough of feeling each other's naked body and stroking each other's slippery cock. At one point, I stuck my finger between Sandy's rounded buns and into his ass. When my finger slipped inside his hot rectum, his sphincter muscles clamped around it and he squirmed all over the rubber sheet.

I'll never know exactly how Woody managed to get his cock into my ass without pushing me all over the place, but when he did it, it felt great. I think Sandy was bracing me from the front, with his tongue licking the salad oil off my balls. As soon as Woody's dick was in me, I let him pump away and I tried to hold his prick inside my ass with my ass muscles. The next thing I knew, he was shooting his wad. I could feel his body jerking and his nuts slamming against me. As soon as he was done, he got off the sheet and went to the fridge and opened a beer. He wiped his feet on a dish towel, then went down the hallway to the linen closet to grab some more towels for drying all of us off.

In the meantime, Sandy and I wriggled up against each other in a sixty-nine, since it seemed that that was the only way we were going to be able to get each other off. It was fun to wriggle and writhe around on the rubber sheet with our bodies so slippery that we couldn't hold onto each other, but it was also frustrating. I wanted to fuck him, and I'm sure he wanted to fuck me. We had to settle for sucking each other off, which was okay, even though fucking would have been better. It was great to feel his slippery smooth body while sucking on his cock and having him suck on mine.

I shot my load before he did, but he wasn't very far behind me. In less than five minutes after Woody had fucked me, Sandy and I had sucked each other off. We used the towels to wipe off most of the oil, then we sat around drinking beers, never getting dressed. I loved sitting around naked with two foxy guys who liked to feel me up and who let me feel them up.

They invited me to spend the night, but when I said I really should go, mentioning my quota again, they offered to make up the difference if I stayed and had sex with them all night long. Sandy said they probably would have spent more than fifty bucks if they had gone out to a bar, which they had planned to do. If I stayed with them, we could have lots of fun, on the rubber sheet and later in bed. They would save money, I would walk away with fifty bucks, and everyone would be happy.

I agreed to do it, because fifty bucks was exactly what I had set out to earn that night.

That evening and that night was great. They fixed some steaks for dinner, and when we weren't having sex, we were drinking beer or wine and feeling each other up. I got to fuck both of them before the night was over, and they fucked me, too. Through the night, none of us slept. Even when we were worn out, someone was always sucking on someone else.

The next morning, they gave me fifty bucks and told me to come back any time. I didn't tell them I was heading out for California. Their offer was tempting, but I was in a hurry to get out of town, before some suspicious customer reported me to the cops. I should have done the same thing when I got to Las Vegas, Nevada. If I had left town when I had the feeling, I wouldn't have ended up in prison. If I had stayed over, if I had gone back to see Woody and Sandy, I would probably have ended up in prison in Oklahoma, and I might never have had the chance to write this story.

KEITH AND THE TRAVELING SALESMAN

Stunning good looks or an athletic body are not necessarily requirements for success when it comes to hustling. In fact, the average street hustler is just that: average. Average height, average build, average looks, average intelligence, and so on. Being called average, however, is not a put-down; it's merely an honest assessment or description. I have a tendency to emphasize a guy's best points and the reader might wonder whether or not all of the guys in this book are for real, since I make each of them sound so great. To me, frankly, each of these is a rare and exquisite young man. But I suppose that if you saw Keith on the street or in the mall or even in the hallway at school, you wouldn't list him in the "gorgeous" column; he's just plain average. Brown hair, blue eyes, and flawed complexion—like most teenagers, he had an acne problem. It wasn't severe enough to earn him the nickname "pizza face"; but even two or three pimples are enough to detract from an otherwise pretty face. I've learned from the numerous young men I've talked to that the men who pick up teenagers are attracted to something more elusive than mere physical beauty. The teenager has lost his innocence, he is no longer a child, and not quite an adult; the teenager is rapidly approaching the peak of his sexual prowess and is acutely aware of his own sexuality; and the teenager embodies a man's rebellious and searching spirit. Most of the pickups are not out to destroy innocence or to force a kid to do something he has no inclination for, because by the time the kid is hustling, he knows damn good and well what he's doing and why. Keith's story is a good example of the genuine concern most pickups feel toward the young strays they help bring out of the cold.

I GREW UP ON a dairy farm in South Dakota. The high school I went to was small, and everyone knew everyone else. Except for me. I don't think anyone knew I existed. I'm quiet and shy.

I never made any friends, because I was always working for my dad on his farm and I never had time for anything else.

I reached puberty when I was twelve, but I never had a chance to experiment with sex with anyone, because there was no one my own age on the farm. I knew I was supposed to be interested in girls, but I wasn't. A farm boy learns a lot about the sexual facts of life from the farm animals and I was no different. My dad owned a couple of black angus bulls which serviced the heifers; but lots of times I caught the bulls fucking each other. So, even though the most common coupling in nature was male and female, the coupling of two males was not unheard of.

My dad never talked about sex, of course; and neither did my mother. They were pretty old fashioned. They figured I would learn what I needed to, just being around the farm animals. But it wasn't the animals I was interested in. We had about half a dozen farm hands, most of the time, and one of them was always especially nice to me. His name was Lefty and he treated me like a man, not like the boss's son. We were alike in a lot of ways, especially in that we were both quiet most of the time.

By the time I was sixteen, I was randy as hell and I knew that I had to have sex pretty soon or I'd end up fucking one of the calves. I had gotten it into my head that Lefty might be like me— he might like boys instead of girls. I don't know where I got that idea, but once it took root, it wouldn't let go. So one day, when Lefty and me were the last two men in the showers before supper, I made the mistake of coming on to him and letting him know that I was interested in him, sexually. I forget how it happened. I just know it was the biggest, stupidest mistake I've ever made. If you don't know for sure, don't push it! I just remember thinking that if one of us didn't say something sooner or later, we'd never get around to doing it together, and I was convinced that Lefty would like it as much as I would. I learned the hard way how wrong I was.

Lefty went straight into the house and told my dad what I'd said and done. My dad beat me within an inch of my life with his razor strop. But I don't think the beating hurt so much as the humiliation. All the farm hands talked about me behind my back, and Lefty never spoke to me again. My mom was mortified by the whole thing and just left it all up to my dad. Dad made it clear that no son of his was ever gonna become no faggot. After that, I could tell that he hated me for what I'd become. I started thinking about leaving home, but I couldn't get up the nerve to leave.

What made up my mind for me about leaving home was all the bullshit I put up with in high school. I'll never know how my classmates eventually found out, but the other guys were teasing me and making fun of me. A couple of them even wanted to beat the shit out of me. In a small farm community, there just ain't no way to hide it, I guess. I thought about killing myself, but deep inside, I didn't really want to die. I just wanted to go somewhere else, so I could just be me.

School was almost out for the year, and a long summer was ahead. I was gonna have to work on the farm with Lefty and the others. I didn't even wait for summer vacation to get there; I just packed a change of clothes in my school back pack, instead of my school books, and when I got to school on one particular Tuesday morning, I just didn't go inside. I knew where my folks hid some cash in the house; so during the night before I left, I went to the hiding place and took enough money for a bus ticket. I knew they wouldn't miss the money until after I was gone.

I had to take a bus, because everyone knew everyone in that part of the state and if anyone was to give me a ride, there'd be lots of questions. I couldn't start hitchhiking until I got out of the state.

I headed south, figuring that I might eventually be able to find a job on a ranch or a farm in Texas. But a long time before I got that far south, I was beginning to find out that there were plenty of others like me in this world; lots of guys who like guys. In fact, most of the rides I got were from men who either came right out and told me they wanted to have sex with me or hinted strongly about it, waiting for me to give them some encouragement.

I'll be honest about it: at first I was scared. The first man to start talking about sex got me wondering whether or not I'd run into some sort of serial killer or something. I had no reason to think that; it's just that I'd only had one previous experience, and it had been a nightmare.

So the first couple of times that someone tried to make a play for me, I acted like I thought it was wrong and sick. They dropped me off at the nearest convenient place to stop and went on without me.

The third guy to bring up sex, though, was real nice about it. He told me that a lot of kids hitchhiked for no other reason. He told me he would like to give me a blowjob and that he would give me some money if I let him do it; but he certainly wasn't going to get pushy if that wasn't my thing. We talked for a long time before I finally gave in. I was glad I did, because (of course) the blowjob felt terrific—it was exactly what the doctor ordered!—and the money came in handy.

It was toward the end of my first day on the road and we stopped at a deserted spot along the highway. All the time he had my pants down and was sucking on my cock, I was scared to death someone was going to pull up beside us and catch us in the act.

He paid me the money and told me he would give me even more if I was to give him a blowjob, too; but I was still too scared. We got back on the highway and sometime long after dark, he dropped me off and went on his way.

I didn't get any more rides that night. I curled up under the overpass at an interchange and spent the night listening to the rumble of cars and trucks. I managed to get a little sleep, but not much.

The next day, I made it as far south as Arkansas, and was again picked up mostly by men who wanted to have sex with me. All in all, I picked up about thirty dollars that day, without having to do anything in return.

By nightfall, I was exhausted. It's not easy hitchhiking, even when sex isn't involved. It's hard to keep up a sociable conversation when you didn't get much sleep the night before. I was just about ready to look for another overpass to sleep under, when I got picked up by a man with a Texas accent. His name was Ray and he told me he was a traveling salesman on his way back home to Austin.

He talked a lot about the traveling salesman business, which he apparently liked a lot.

"Sales is one of the most honest professions in the world," he insisted. "When a man wants or needs something, he goes out and buys it. The salesman provides whatever it is he needs and charges a fair price. What can be more honest?" he asked me.

I just sat there and listened to him.

"You take doctors and lawyers, though," he continued. "A lawyer'll charge you up the poop shoot, then won't do nothing but finagle a deal with the other side. Takes fifty percent of your money and didn't do shit. A doctor'll charge you a hundred bucks just to tell you to take two aspirin and call him in the morning." He carried on about doctors and lawyers for a long time, before coming back to the point he was driving at.

"But honest trade is something a man can do and still look himself in the mirror. For example, you've got something I want, I'm willing to pay for it. Or, I've got something you want, you're willing to perform some service for it. If two people agree that the service and the money are equitable, then both parties is happy. That's the way things oughta be."

Eventually, he got around to sex.

"Let's hit a little closer to home," he said. "Let's say you was to need money, 'cause you're broke and ain't got no way to earn a livelihood. You ain't got no product to sell, and there's not too many services you can perform. Now you run into someone like me. I've got plenty of money and I'm willing to pay someone like you to perform certain services. Are you beginning to catch my drift, young fella?"

"I think so," I answered, even though I still wasn't positive that he was talking about sex.

"Well, then; I've wasted enough time beating around the bush; so let me come right out with it. I'm gonna be pulling into a motel up here pretty quick, and I'd like to be able to have a young man like yourself spend the night with me in that motel room. I'm willing to pay for that service. Now, you have to realize that there's more to it than just sleeping. I think you catch my drift. But here's the deal: you've got something I want, and I've got something you need. You need money, and I'm willing to pay you handsomely for what I have in mind. On the other hand, you've got to be willing to perform the services I have in mind. Services that only a fine young man like yourself can render. Are we communicating clearly, here?"

I didn't answer right away, because I truly didn't know what he would expect of me—in bed, that is. Except for the nitty gritty particulars, I was pretty sure I knew what he was talking about.

"Well, sir, you drive a hard bargain," he said with a little bit of a laugh. "Tell you what I'm gonna do. I'm gonna give you a five dollar bill just to break the ice and get things started. But you realize that if I give you something, I want something in return?"

"I guess so."

"Well, then; here's the thing. I'll give you five dollars just to let me feel your *thing* down there. That's all, just feel it. Here's the five bucks."

He pulled out a five dollar bill and pressed it into my hand.

When I didn't make any move to give it back to him, he stretched a little bit further my direction and fumbled for the zipper in my pants. He continually looked up at the road while taking my cock out of my jeans. I tried to keep it from getting hard, because I didn't want to seem to be too anxious, but it felt good the way he held it and felt it.

"Well, there," he said. "You see? We both liked that a lot. And we both got something out of it. That's what I'm talking about. An honest exchange."

He played with my dick for a few minutes, then let go and told me I could put it away. "Now, wasn't that easy?"

"Yeah."

"I'm a fair man; never screwed nobody out of nothin'. Here's what I'll do. I'll hire you for the night. Now that means I'll be your employer, and when you work for a boss, you gotta do what the boss says or he'll fire you, right? Now I know you don't wanta get fired; so all you gotta do is follow orders. Won't be hard. Not like hard work or nothin'. You wanta come to work for me?"

"I guess so," I said, still unsure.

"Don't worry, son; I won't have you doin' nothing to hurt yourself. But listen, youngster: you haven't learned your lesson, yet. You and I ain't come to an agreement on price, yet. You don't figure to have sex with me for just five bucks, do you?"

"Well, no. But I don't know what to charge."

"Name a price," he told me.

I thought about it for a few minutes, but didn't know how much I should charge for spending the whole night with him. Finally, I said, "Twenty dollars?" Then I quickly upped the ante. "I mean, thirty dollars."

He said, "Son, don't ever sell yourself cheap. Let's call a spade a spade. The only thing you've got what's of any value is that young body of yours. It's worth more than twenty or thirty bucks a night. I'll offer you fifty, even though it's probably worth even more than that. What say?"

Worth even more than fifty? How was I to know? Right then and there, fifty bucks seemed like a lot of money. We sealed the bargain with a handshake, and about fifteen minutes later, he pulled off the freeway into the parking lot of a large, expensive looking motel. I don't remember which one it was, but it was one of the big chains. Holiday Inn, Howard Johnson, or one of those.

He had me come into the lobby with him, because he wanted the people to think I was his son and that we were just travelling together. He ordered a room with two beds, so no one would think we were going to sleep together, and he called me son several times. I just played along and stayed quiet, mostly.

Then he asked the desk clerk where the nearest pizza parlor was, and asked me if I wanted to get something to eat, son?

Over pizza, he told me that dinner and breakfast were included in the deal. He reminded me that we'd shook, and when we got back to the motel, I was to follow his orders from the minute the door closed behind us. He again assured me that there wouldn't be nothing weird, just good old fashioned sex between two men.

Back at the motel, as soon as he closed the door, he told me to strip out of my clothes and go on in and get a shower. "I'll be right behind you. We're gonna wash each other's backs." He winked at me and said, "And each other's fronts. We're gonna get to know each other, son. We're gonna start by looking at each other naked under the shower, and we're gonna wash each other's private parts. That way, when we get to doing things a little bit later, won't nothing be a surprise for either one of us. Okay?"

I nodded and started taking my shoes off. He went back out to the car and brought in a suitcase. I was just getting ready to get out of my underwear when he came back into the room.

"That's the way, son. Now, don't be nervous. Before the night's over, we're gonna see each other naked most of the time. Go on ahead and get out of them shorts. Don't be shy; remember, I've already played with the big fella down there; even seen him, although it was dark when I did."

He opened his suitcase and pulled out a flask of whiskey. He took a swig from the flask, then held it out toward me. "You're too young to drink, but I figure a short snort can't hurt much. Want one?"

Standing in front of him, I was aware of his eyes scanning my body, mostly the area of my dick. I took the flask and pulled a long swallow on it. I immediately gasped and choked, but managed not to spit any of it out. It felt good going down and I thanked him for it. I gave the flask back and turned to go into the bathroom.

"God, them's some nice young buns you got there, son!"

I ignored the praise and went on into the bathroom where I wasted no time getting under the hot running water. The shower was over the tub and was enclosed by frosted glass sliding doors. The water felt so good, since I hadn't had a bath in three days.

About five minutes after I got into the shower, one of the glass doors slid open and Ray's naked body stepped into the tub. I couldn't help but make a mental comparison between the two of us. I was young; he was middle-aged: maybe fifty. I was about five-eight or five-nine; he was six-one or six-two. I weighed maybe one-fifty; he was probably about one-ninety, 'cause he wasn't overweight. My body was completely hairless, except for my arm-pits and my pubic area; Ray's body was covered with a thick car-pet of curly brown and grey hair (but not on his back, I noticed). I had always thought of myself as being of average build, but I guess years of hard work on my dad's farm contributed to some pretty hard muscles, even though they weren't very big or well de-fined; Ray was muscular in a ropy, lanky sort of way. We both had big hands and big feet for out relative sizes. I remember think-ing how big and strong his hands were when he'd been playing with my dick in the car.

"Sorry to keep you waiting," he said, sliding past me, feeling and holding my slippery body as he did so. "Let me get wet all over. I had a couple things to take care of before we got started."

He opened the sliding glass door at his end and reached out for one of the courtesy bars of soap and a wash cloth. He lathered up the cloth. I was facing him, but his body was blocking most of the shower spray. He stepped right up to me and began to swish the cloth around over my chest and stomach, then he care-fully soaped up my dick and my balls.

"Yessir, that's one nice lookin' piece of meat you got there, young man. Respectable for one your size. What do you think of mine, huh?"

The thing about Ray was that he seemed to talk non-stop. I couldn't begin to try to repeat everything he said. But it's interesting that he never seemed to get on my nerves. He was likable and friendly. Talking just sort of seemed to kill the silence between us, which would have lingered forever, if it had been up to me. If I don't know what to say, I don't say it; so most of the time, I kept my mouth shut.

I let him soap me up real good, bracing myself by holding onto his left arm while he shoved his big right arm between my legs and washed my nuts and my ass, then down my legs. He had me turn around and he scrubbed some more. It felt really good, the way he lathered up the rag, then soaped me up with it. When he washed my neck and shoulders, he put a lot of pressure into it and it was like getting a massage.

When he handed me the cloth, we swapped places and I stood with my back to the stream of water. I washed him the same way he'd done me, and he kept up a running monologue all the while, usually complimenting me on my body, or on my fine ass, or on my commendable piece of meat, or on my pretty blue eyes, or on the way I soaped him up real good, or the way I was careful not to hurt his nuts when I soaped between his legs, and so on. It was a little bit embarrassing, but it was also kind of nice. I'd never had anyone treat me so nice before. It was nice to know that someone really thought I was good looking, even though I know I'm really not as "gorgeous" as he called me. Under the hot water of that shower, I developed a warm feeling for Ray; I really started liking him real well.

This "getting to know each other party," as he called it, was fun and it felt good. We did more than just wash each other, we felt and played with and looked and rubbed. At first, I hadn't liked all his hair; but by the time we were through, I found it kind of neat. I thought of him as a skinny teddy bear or something. And at the same time, he made me glad that I was so smooth. I had always been self-conscious about my inability to grow much hair. I still grew peach fuzz on my face and I wondered if I'd ever develop any hair on my chest—a situation which my dad had always equated with being "a man." Ray's body was soft and furry; my body was soft and slippery. It was a nice combination.

After rinsing off, we got out of the tub and Ray dried me off with a thick towel, sometimes rubbing vigorously, sometimes blotting gently. He really knew how to make a guy feel good all over.

Back in the main room, he told me to lie down on one of the two queen-size beds. "You'll be sleeping with me," he said. "We'll both sleep in one bed; but we gotta make it look like we used both. So, we'll use both. Lay down there. I'm gonna make you feel all soft and smooth."

He had brought a second suitcase from his car while I was waiting for him in the shower. It held all sorts of things we would need as the night wore on, like baby powder and Vaseline. I also noticed that he had brought in my back pack, which I'd tossed into the back seat when I got into his car earlier that evening. I was glad he'd done that, because I wanted to put on clean clothes in the morning, after having worn the same things for two full days.

He'd brought a dry towel from the bathroom with him and he told me to keep it under me at all times. "If and when either one of us shoots a load, we want to try to keep it off the spread. Not that we care about the spread, itself; we just don't want the maids to know we was shooting jizz all over the place, now, do we!"

He had me lie on my stomach and he sprinkled baby powder all over me, then rubbed it in. My mom hadn't used powder on me since I was too little to remember, and now when Ray sprinkled it on and rubbed it in, it felt wonderfully soft and smooth. He started at my shoulders and worked his way slowly down my back. He talked all the time about how pretty my body was and how smooth.

"Yessir, I'm definitely getting the better part of this bargain. But now, listen; when you're doing business with someone, don't ever let on that you'd be willing to go higher, like I'm doing here. That wouldn't be good business sense."

He slowly sprinkled the powder over my buns and lovingly smeared it all over. He took longer with my buns than with any other part of my body.

"The bargaining that you and me done in the car is a prime example of what not to do and say. When I asked you to name a price, you said twenty, then jumped it to thirty. Never do that. Always start high, 'cause then you can come down; but y'ain't supposed to go up, like I let you."

He powdered my legs while he was talking, but quickly came back to my now baby-soft ass. "And me: I ain't supposed to offer you more'n you ask, like I did. But I know you're new at this; so I just couldn't bring myself to cheat you. You'll get the hang of it, and who knows you might even decide to go into sales when you grow up."

For a moment he seemed lost in what he was doing. His fingers were working the powder between the cheeks of my ass. With his large fingers, he spread my buttocks apart, then I heard him sigh. "Lord, what a sweet, delicate little ass you got there. You a virgin, young man?"

I said I was.

"You runnin' away from home?"

"Yeah. You're not gonna turn me in, are you?"

"Lord no! I believe it's healthy for a young man to break the apron strings. I, myself, ran away when I was just a puppy. I believe a man's gotta sort this old world out for himself, with a little help along the way from people with more experience."

He had me roll over, then before applying powder, he felt my body and ran his fingers down to my pubic hairs. He scratched my groin area for a moment with manicured fingernails. "You certainly are young," he said, with a far-away sound in his voice. He then quickly sprinkled more powder all over my front and gently eased it into my skin. I was in seventh heaven, it felt so good.

He then asked me to powder him up, and I followed the same general motions and sequence as he'd gone through. When he was on his back, with his hard cock jutting straight up and away from his groin, and I was rubbing powder all over his nuts, he grabbed me and pulled me on top of him.

He kissed me a lot and glided his hands over my powdery smooth back-side while rubbing our cocks together. Then he rolled me over and positioned himself on top of me. He squeezed my legs together by placing his legs outside of mine. Then he slipped his long, hard cock between my legs, just below my nuts. I could feel it slide past my nutsac, close to my ass, as he went in and out, up and down. He was fucking me between the legs, the powder allowing his thick piece of meat to pass back and forth without too much friction. He continued to kiss me a lot, breathing hard and moaning and sighing like he was hurting. But he wasn't hurt, he was feeling pretty damned good. He humped and pumped and bounced us up and down on the bed till I thought the neighbors could hear on both sides. When I said something about it, Ray assured me that the walls were thick enough to cover up any such sounds.

Then he rammed his stiff cock between my legs with such force that I knew he'd reached orgasm. His body jerked and writhed and twisted and shivered like a snake trying to get out from under a forked twig. He thrashed until I thought he was gonna crush me, but he finally calmed down and then just sort of went limp on top of me.

In a couple of minutes, he got up and pulled the towel out from under me. "We'll get another one in a minute," he said. He threw it in a corner and went to the nightstand which held his flask and had another swig, then offered me one. I accepted and we talked (or I should say *he* talked) for a few more minutes. Then he told me he wanted me to fuck him. Not the way he'd done me; he wanted me to fuck him in the ass, for real.

"When I figured you was a virgin, I said to myself that I wasn't gonna be the one to take advantage of you. Not unless you want me to. I'll let you make that decision later. We've got all night and into the morning. But for right now, I want to be the first person you fuck. I'd be proud to be the first ass you shove your dick up into."

He told me to smear some Vaseline on my dick and to put a little bit on his ass. He lay flat on his stomach and told me to climb on top and go at it. I positioned myself above Ray's body, with my legs between his and with my arms extended and my elbows locked in place. For a man his age, Ray had a fairly nice body; his back was strong and he didn't have much of a middle-age spread. His buns were still firm and nicely rounded. From the back, he actually looked a lot younger.

I hovered above his body, looking down on him with an excitement and expectation that I couldn't explain. My cock was pointed at his ass and it was throbbing so bad I wanted to grab it and jack off; but I knew something better was coming. So I just pressed forward until my dick touched the part in his cheeks. I didn't know if I was supposed to use my hand to put my cock in his rectum, or if I was just supposed to push my dick past his cheeks until it slipped into the opening. I found that my dick slid into his ass real easy, with only a little push. But his ass muscles presented just enough resistance to create a wild sensation along the length of my cock as it slid deeper into his hot, moist interior. The feeling was incredibly exciting! Jacking off never felt so good. Those handjobs and blowjobs I got while hitchhiking were nothing by comparison.

Slipping my cock through his tight ass muscles and into the hot, slippery insides of his asshole sent a tingle through my cock that didn't stop there. It went all the way up my spine and into my head. I shivered with the pleasure of it, and I let out a loud sigh, just as Ray had done.

Having successfully plunged my swollen piece of meat into his hot body, I unlocked my elbows and lowered myself onto his powder-dusted back. Our powdery bodies slipped against each other with such softness and warmth that the delicate feelings in my arms and chest transferred themselves down to my cock and I found myself thrusting my cock as deeply as it would go.

There is no way to describe the very first time you push your cock past the sphincter muscles of someone's ass and feel the rim of muscles tighten against your shaft as you penetrate into the fleshy cave. There's no sense in even trying to come up with the words. All I can say is, it was mind-boggling. It wasn't just my dick that felt all the sensations, either; it seemed like my whole body was involved. Even my toes curled down; my thighs felt like they were on fire; my face felt hot; my own ass muscles twitched and contracted. And the fact that both of our bodies were covered with baby powder merely added to the sensual pleasures and heightened the feeling of flesh on flesh, and flesh *in* flesh.

It didn't take me long to cum. My body was experiencing things I'd never felt before and the moment of orgasm had been building since he first reached into my jeans in his car and pulled out my dick to play with it. The time which elapsed between my putting it back in my pants and then getting into the shower with him had only been a slight delay; from the moment of the shower forward, my body had been preparing for the onset of a dynamic explosion. And now that eruption was upon me.

I felt the moment of climax surging inside my balls and I began to beat my dick fiercely inside Ray's ass. Back and forth, across the firm ass muscles, my cock pounded in and out. Then, with a shock-like convulsion, my whole body felt as if it would come apart with the shattering effect of the orgasm. I gripped Ray's shoulders tightly, and I squeezed my legs together powerfully, while I thrust my mid-section into his buns. Explosion after explosion of hot sperm shot through my cock and my body jerked with each new eruption, until finally I collapsed in a heap on his back.

I felt as if I couldn't move. My body was trembling, from head to toes, and I was panting so hard I thought I was going to suffocate; but my muscles wouldn't respond to my will to roll off him. Ray didn't seem to mind that I was just laying on top of him, my dick still embedded in his ass. I loved the warm feel of his body beneath me, and of the powder which made us both feel so soft. Ray was in no hurry for me to get off, and his hands wrapped behind him and over me, feeling what he could manage to reach of my silky smooth body.

At last, I felt my dick beginning to lose some of its hardness; so I slowly backed out of his ass. When the head plopped through, I rolled over to the side and lay there, spread eagle, exhausted and happy. It had been the most remarkable experience in all of my life. The only thing that came close to it was the very first orgasm I ever had, and I knew I would never forget that.

Ray turned on his side and ran his fingers over my body, feeling me up and making me feel good all over. "We'll have some more fun, later," he said, taking another swig from his flask. "Let's take a break and watch some TV."

He wiped my cock clean with one of the motel towels and reapplied powder to my entire groin area. He turned on the large color TV and located a movie channel, then pulled one of the arm chairs over from the writing table and set it between the two beds. He asked me to sit on his lap while we watched a movie, and I gladly did as he asked.

While we watched the movie, his cock was nestled firmly between my buns in the crack of my ass and our naked bodies touched several places. I reached down to scratch my nuts and grabbed a handful of his cock. It gave us both a bit of a surprise, but it felt good, nonetheless. He held me on his lap, constantly feeling my body and playing with my dick.

I don't think either one of us was paying any attention to the movie (in fact, I can't even remember what it was). Neither one of us was ready to have sex again right away, but it was wonderfully pleasant to sit on his lap, naked flesh against naked flesh, his hands always moving, always feeling, always making me feel like a king. No one, in my entire life, had ever paid me that much attention. It felt good. It felt like I was the only person in his life who mattered. He made me feel important. He made me feel good about myself.

Half way through a second movie, neither one of us could hardly keep our eyes open; so we decided to call it a night. I helped him polish off the remains of the whiskey in the flask and we crawled into one of the queen size beds. I backed up to him and he held me close to his warm body. Within a very short time, we were both so horny we couldn't sleep.

We played around with each other for about an hour and ended up in a sixty-nine, sucking each other off, under the covers. It was great. My body had never felt so alive.

We finally got to sleep and morning came all too soon. One of the things in his suitcase was an alarm clock which shattered through my dreams. Ray was horny from the moment he woke up, and I guess I have to admit that so was I. After working me up to a state of high sexual excitement, he made me get out of bed and we finished in the shower, sucking each other off under the hot, steamy water. That guy Ray showed me some fantastic experiences. I was beginning to dread having to leave him and hit the road again. It had been great, all of it.

True to his promise, he took me for breakfast. Over pancakes and sausages, he asked me if I had any idea where I was going.

I told him truthfully that I didn't really care. Maybe Texas; maybe the west coast. He told me he'd take me as far as Austin, if I chose to go there. I could then go on to San Antonio where I could catch the interstate going west, if I wanted, or I could get out in Dallas. All I had to do was let him know.

I decided to go all the way to Austin with him, even though he had to make several business stops along the way. That meant that he would have to stay in a motel, again, in Dallas before hitting the final leg of his homeward journey.

And you guessed it, he told me to name my price for another night of wild sex with him.

That second night, I decided to let him fuck me. I couldn't understand what the big deal was about being fucked, until he actually did it. It definitely takes some getting used to; but I'm glad Ray was the one to teach me how to do it right.

I eventually did a lot of street hustling through Texas, hitting most of the major cities, going wherever I could make a few bucks turning a trick. I learned the hard way that I was too young to get any kind of a job that paid much of anything; so I deliberately misinterpreted what Ray told me, and I went into "sales"—selling my body for the best price I could get for it.

I met a lot of people along the way, but I never found anyone I liked nearly so much as Ray. The day after he and I parted company, I found an extra fifty bucks in my back-pack, with a little note that said, "Never sell yourself short."

BRENT AND GETTING PAID FOR HAVING FUN

Of the many stories in this book, only a couple involve kids who did not run away from home. What this tells us, basically, is that most of the guys on Vaseline Alley are there because they've got nowhere else to go and no one to help them. Brent, on the other hand, is one of the few who took to male prostitution because he liked sex. How many adolescents get the chance to indulge in unlimited sex? How many opportunities are there for teenagers to satisfy their overwhelming urges and uncontrollable desires? Brent was a skinny kid with straight, long, brown hair and large, round brown eyes. When I met him, he was tall and lanky; but he tells me he didn't shoot up until he was almost twenty years old! When he was in his early teens, he was a little runt of a kid, and even when this story took place, he was a very small eighteen year old who looked years younger than his actual age. He was, however, endowed with a dick like a fire hose, and he couldn't get enough sex from the very first time he got a hardon. His cock outdistanced him when he began ripening into a teenager, and there was only one safe way to try to quell his unquenchable thirst for orgasm: prostitution. For Brent, the money didn't matter, even though he never turned it down; all that mattered was sex, sex, sex.

I GREW UP with my dad in a trailer house. My mom ran off with some guy when I was too young to remember. Trailer houses aren't great for privacy, and it's rough on a kid when he starts jacking off, because if his dad's home, there's no way of hiding what you're doing.

When I was eleven, I started getting interested in guys and in sex and my cock started growing. I was whacking my pud before I was able to grow hair down there. But I could never satisfy my craving for the hot rush of an orgasm. Six or seven times a day was never enough for me, and that's no bullshit. I've slowed down over the years, but even now I've got to get a nut at least three or four times a day, and I like to jack off in risky places, where I take a chance of being caught, like in public restrooms, or on the bus with my coat in my lap. Shit like that.

My dad worked swing shift, most of the time; so he usually wasn't home. My problem, as a teenager, was that jacking off gets old. I needed to have sex with another hot body. By the time I was fifteen, I had approached any boy my own age who showed half an interest in a little sex play. Then, one day I met a guy at the video arcade and brought him home with me. I talked him into playing a make-believe game of *Wizards*, or something stupid like that. I tied him up in my dad's bedroom and began taking his clothes off of him, one piece at a time. I pretended he was an enemy captive and that I was torturing him for secrets, or something. The only real torture involved me playing with his dick and not getting him off until he got me off, and with my cock poor Andy's mouth took a lot of punishment.

Andy played along pretty good and we had a blast. He liked sex almost as much as I did. We switched back and forth playing the Master and the Slave.

One day, Andy told me how he got picked up by a guy who paid him to have sex with him. He then told me that it happens a lot and he took me to a certain block in the run-down part of town where other boys hung out, waiting to get picked by guys willing to pay for sex.

I found it hard to believe that people would actually want to pay me to have sex! Hell, I was willing to *pay them* for it! So I went with Andy down to what he called Vaseline Alley and I hung out. I got to know most of the other guys who hung out there, after awhile. Most of them were younger than me. I couldn't believe how young some of them were. Most of them, though, were like me: they liked sex. To me, making money wasn't the important thing; having sex was. To these other guys, though, it was important to them to turn tricks for money. That's how they supported themselves.

Because making money was more important to them than it was to me, I usually held back and let them take the tricks. I made myself available only when the other guys had already scored. Frankly, I liked it better when I took one of them home with me, because most of the customers were sort of boring. Quickie handjobs, quickie blowjobs. Where's the excitement? I liked going home to my dad's trailer and playing wild sex games with these guys. They knew how to have fun.

One night, though, a guy picked me up in a sports car and after talking things over at curbside, I agreed to go with him up to the lake. I yelled back to Andy, who was standing in a doorway, and told him I was going to the lake. He warned me not to go; but I felt okay with this guy. I had the feeling that he wasn't going to hurt me, and that he definitely wasn't going to be a bore.

We stopped at a 7-11 and he bought a case of beer, a roll of paper towels, some Vaseline, and several bags of chips and things.

The lake was about fifteen miles from town. There were lots of places where you could park and not be seen, especially in the off-season (like right then). There were boat ramps, picnic areas, campfire areas, and all kinds of other places surrounded by trees, shrubs, closed-down snack bars, restrooms, and so on.

The guy in the sports car, whose name was Joel, tooled around the mountain roads for about half an hour, treating me to the special talents of his Corvette. Then he pulled into one of the more remote picnic areas, on what we called the backside of the lake. The sun was down by the time we set the beer, chips, and other stuff on the old redwood table, which was only fifty feet from the water's edge. Even though it was early spring, the weather was nice and the lake looked calm and mild.

Joel told me he was forty-four years old. He was gay, of course; his lover had died several years back. Since that time, he had not gotten involved with anyone in any kind of special relationship. The pain of his loss was still too heavy. One of his older friends had told him about Vaseline Alley, where he could pick up guys for the sole purpose of having sex—no involvements, no attachments, no relationships. He thought about it for a long time before he finally took the plunge. I just happened to be the first guy he had dared to stop and talk to, even though he had driven by that area several times.

He wanted to talk for awhile, 'cause he was curious about what it was like being a hustler, and so on.

I answered his questions to the best of my ability. When I told him I was eighteen, he didn't believe me. My body was still pretty small, back then, and I guess I looked like I was maybe fourteen or fifteen, or something.

He told me I was still the youngest guy he had ever had sex with. He had never been interested in kids under the legal age. When he picked me up, he was afraid I wasn't really old enough, but he liked what he saw and decided to go for it. He was glad that I was eighteen.

After two beers for him and one for me, and a bag of tortilla chips between the two of us, he loosened up and took his shirt off. I did the same. He commented on how skinny I was, then said, "But I like it that way. You're really very sexy for a kid."

Joel wasn't too bad, himself, considering he was older than my own father. He had a full head of hair, a nice chest with lots of wiry hair on it, and a waist line on which he probably had to work hard to keep it that small. There was only a hint of tummy flab, which on most other men would have already turned into a spare tire.

"Wanta go skinny dipping?" I asked him.

He looked at me all crazy like, then laughed and said, "Yeah, what the fuck! Why not? No one can sneak up on us without us hearing the sound of their engine, and I got a blanket and some towels in the trunk. Let's go for it."

We couldn't help but look at each other's body as we took our clothes off. When he saw my dick, he said, "Damn! How'd a little kid like you get a tube of salami like that?"

"I told you I wasn't no kid! Now do you believe me?"

We were standing right next to each other. He reached out and took ahold of my cock. Just the feel of it made his own cock start to throbbing. "That cold water will make our dicks shrivel up," he said. "Maybe we should take care of other things first. Like these fuckpoles of ours."

We went to his 'Vette and got the blanket and towels out of the trunk. He stuffed them into my arms, then picked me up and carried me back to the table. I'd never had sex with anyone so much bigger and stronger than me. It was neat having him carry me, like that, my naked body in his strong arms. Back at the table, he set me down and I spread the blanket, letting it drape down over the side and onto the bench. Joel reached into the bag of groceries and pulled out the jar of Vaseline.

"Have you ever been fucked in the ass?" he asked.

"Lots of times," I told him.

"The next question is: how many assholes have you torn wide open with that power tool of yours?"

I laughed and told him that I had never fucked anyone with it, because it was so big and I was afraid I'd hurt someone.

"Well, this is my party and I want to fuck; so I'm gonna fuck you first, but afterwards, I'm gonna try to take that baseball bat of yours up my ass. I love a big cock up my ass; but I'll admit I've never had one that big, before. I never thought the biggest cock I'd ever see would belong to a kid."

He sat down next to me on the table, our feet touching the blanket-covered bench. He was sitting on my left, and he wrapped his right arm around my shoulder. He lightly rubbed me all over my back, down to the crack of my ass cheeks, then brought his hand back to my shoulder and pulled my body closer to him. He bent me over his knee, as if he was going to spank me.

There I was, sprawled across his lap, my cock pressing against his right thigh, and his cock sticking up against my stomach. For a split second, I thought he was going to get kinky on me. But then I saw him dip his fingers into the jar of Vaseline. Next thing I knew, the thick lubricant was being smeared around my asshole. I've got a special feeling for that! I love it when someone plays with my ass, especially if he's smearing lotion or oil. I like it smeared all over my buns and even down under, between my legs and onto my balls. I told this to Joel and he obliged me by smearing the Vaseline all over my buns, making them feel silky as hell, then he smeared some more between my legs.

He made me get up and stand in front of him while he scooted down to the bench. He was sitting there in front of me, his cock sticking straight up. He told me he wanted me to sit down on it, facing him.

He handed me the Vaseline and told me to smear it all over his cock. Joel's cock felt really neat while I was putting Vaseline all over it. It was hard, thick, and so soft, too. While I was getting his cock ready to penetrate my ass, Joel was fondling my meat. He was using just one hand, though, and I liked for a guy to use both hands when stroking me off.

I put the Vaseline down and stepped over the bench with my right leg. Before stepping over with my left leg, I bunched up the blanket behind him. Then I sat down directly on top of his cock and wrapped my arms and legs around him. I lifted my butt and let him angle his stiff piece of meat into my asshole. It was so hard and so soft at the same time that when it touched my ass muscles, it gave me two different sensations. I was afraid it was going to hurt like hell when he started, but then when he pushed, it felt wildly soft and pliant, sliding in easily because of the Vaseline.

He held on to me by the waist, his big hands almost completely encircling my narrow body.

I lowered my body onto his fucktool and felt him pushing upward at the same time. As soon as I was firmly planted on his dick, he scooted forward on the redwood bench and then took hold of my dick with both hands, the way I like it. I started bouncing up and down, riding him like a rocking horse, while he pumped my cock back and forth.

He let go of my dick and wrapped his arms around me, pulling me close enough to kiss. We kissed each other for a long time. He sucked hard on my tongue and I wondered what it would be like to get a blowjob from him.

His hands were feeling me up all over, down my legs, up my back, and down my chest and arms. I pressed closer to him while rocking up and down on his cock, trying to get my dick to press against his stomach. I needed to feel something on the head of my fuck shaft, even if it was nothing but the smooth flesh of his abdomen.

His fingertips dug into my buns as he approached his orgasm, and I could tell he was getting there fast because of the way we were rocking back and forth and up and down. On one of my upward strokes, he grabbed my buns tightly, forcing his hands between my buns and his thighs. He got a firm handhold and I thought he was ready to pop a nut; but to my surprise, he stood up from the bench, lifting me up with him, his cock embedded in my ass. I wrapped my legs around him again and kept my body bent at just the right angle for him to keep his dick inside me.

He began to walk around with me impaled on his dick, like that, and the walking motion continued the pumping of his meat up my ass. It felt really wild!

Then he jerked forward and I thought he was going to fall, or drop me, or both. But he just kept walking, plowing his thick cock into my ass with each jerk of his body. He was hitting his orgasm as he walked, his cock pouring hot jizz into my ass with each step he took. A few more times, I could have sworn he was going to fall, but he was strong enough to hold on to me, even though his knees felt like they were going to buckle out from under him.

He walked around the picnic table, while his cock squirted again and again. Even when he had finished emptying his hot cream into my rectum, he continued to walk with his cock in my ass, until he had circled the table completely. He set me down on the end of the table. Only then did his cock slide out of my ass.

I had never had anyone do anything like that before. It was totally unreal! It felt fantastic and I've wanted to try the same thing with someone else, with me doing the walking and holding on to his buns. But I have a hard time trying to find anyone who'll let me fuck him, let alone walk around with him impaled on my monster shaft like that.

"Now it's your turn," he said breathlessly, panting and moaning. "I want to try to take that monster of yours up my ass. Let's spread the blanket near the water. The sandy beach will be better than the hard ground right here."

Near the lake edge, he spread the blanket out and lay down on his stomach, with his legs spread apart for easy access to his ass. It was a cloudless night and his muscular buns looked beautiful in the pale moonlight. I had brought the Vaseline jar; so I crawled between his legs and applied a generous amount of the thick lotion to his ass, then smeared a large gob of it on my cock. I positioned myself on top of him where my dick was lined up with his asshole. I was hot and horny, my tube throbbing, and I was afraid I might cum prematurely, even before I got it all the way up his ass.

He warned me to go slow, and even though I wanted to ram it in and just start hammering away, I knew he wouldn't be able to handle it that way. The slick feel of his lubed up buns against the head of my dick sent a shiver of excitement through me and I pressed forward. When I felt the resistance of his ass muscles, I stopped for a moment.

Hovering over him. as if I was going to do push-ups, I slowly pushed my cock against his ass. I could tell he was doing everything possible to loosen up; but even so, I had to gently force my cock past the tight little knot of muscles. Joel was no virgin, and he knew how to use his ass; but getting my thick pole in was going to be a real test of will. He might change his mind about wanting my huge piece of meat up his ass. Like I said before, the size of my cock has presented some real problems in the past. I like having a big cock, but sometimes I wish it had been just a little bit smaller.

I pulled back and applied some more Vaseline to my prick, then took aim again. This time, when my dickhead pressed against his sphincter, I pushed a little harder. He moaned softly and I stopped, but he told me to keep on going.

I pushed some more and felt the head of my cock moving past the muscles. He groaned louder, but I continued to push, gently but firmly. Then I felt the head plop past the opening. The head of my dick is as big as the shaft; so I knew we were past the point of no return.

I began a deliberate push, all the way in, non-stop, but ever so slowly. I was genuinely amazed by the feel of slipping my dick into someone's ass. The feeling was indescribable. I dug my toes into the sand and continued to push.

"Oh, God, I don't think I can take it," he moaned.

"It's almost all the way in," I said, not wanting to pull out. God, I didn't want him to stop me! Not after I'd gotten that far. It would only take me a minute to shoot my load, then I could pull out. But you've got to realize that I had wanted to know what it felt like to fuck someone for too many years! Now that my cock was shoved deep into a hot ass, I didn't want to stop.

He said it again, and I was afraid he was going to tell me to pull it out; so I lowered myself onto his back and lay motionless on top of him for a few minutes.

"I don't know which feels best," he said, "when you stop or when you do it. My ass feels like you're tearing me apart, but having that huge piece of meat inside me feels like heaven. I'd like to get used to it."

Slowly, I began to pull back out, but then reversed course and pushed in again. He moaned, but didn't complain; so I kept on going. Then I began to pick up speed. I made long, slow strokes, sliding my huge pole up and down along the length of his rectum, hoping that the Vaseline was managing to ease any pain he might be feeling.

He reached one of his hands around behind his back and slid it between our bodies. I was gaining speed and enjoying the high of having my cock slide in and out, squeezed by the tightness of his ass muscles. I knew it wasn't going to take me long to catch a nut, because the sensations were greater than anything I'd ever felt before. His hand was sliding down between our bodies and getting closer to my pubic hair, just above my pumping cock. When his fingernails scratched the insides of my thighs next to my nuts, I felt the surge of sperm rushing into the head of my dick.

The feel of my cock in his ass was wild and I felt more sexual than I'd ever felt. I groaned loudly when the first load of cum erupted from my cock into the deep recesses of his rectum. I shuddered and trembled and shot another load, while my body contracted with frantic jerking. The cum kept emptying out of me, causing my cock to plunge deeper into his ass, deeper than I had planned on going. He let out a yelp, but it was followed by what sounded like a loud sigh of pleasure.

When I was through pumping cum into his hot ass, I knew I had to pull out fast or I'd have to stay inside him until I came a second time. And I wasn't sure he could take any more; not for awhile. I pulled out so quick that all he could do was gasp.

I rolled over to his side and lay there panting. I had finally done it. I had finally fucked someone in the ass. I was ready to do it again, but there was no way Joel could handle it. For several minutes, he just lay still, moaning and talking about how good it had felt. When he finally got up and went to the table to get a couple of beers, I couldn't help but stroke my cock, because I was still horny. When he got back, we drank the beers; then I asked him to jack me off. Using both hands, the way I like it, he brought me to another climax in just a couple of minutes.

Before getting up, I asked him if he was ready to shoot a second load, and he said he wouldn't be able to cum again until his body recuperated. So we drank some more beer and ate some more chips. The night started getting colder.

Before packing it in for the night, we had sex again. He shot his load one more time and managed to suck me off without hurting his mouth too bad; then he let me fuck him between the legs. When we were both exhausted, we climbed into his 'Vette and headed back to town.

I had him drop me off at the entrance to the trailer park I lived in, so I wouldn't have to walk all the way back home from downtown. It was almost ten o'clock, and before my dad got home from work, I took a hot shower and whacked my pud one more time, thinking about how great it had been to fuck someone in the ass.

Then I thought about the money, and I shook my head in amazement that people would actually pay me for having sex with them. The customers I picked up didn't realize how badly I needed to have sex. I'm like a junkie; I can't get along without it. It was ironic that I should be getting paid for having so much fun.

RUSTY AND
THE SPECTATOR

The names I use in this book are fictitious, for obvious reasons. Most of the time, there is no particular reason to pick one name over another. In Rusty's case, however, I simply couldn't resist using this name because of the kid's hair color. To say he has red hair is putting it mildly. The words auburn and copper don't do it justice. No; Rusty's hair was the color of oxidized iron—rust. And his hair was so thick, you could barely run your fingers through it. I don't think he ever had to comb it; it possessed a natural curliness and it seemed eternally set in one style. And in case you're wondering, yes: his pubes were the same rusty color. His eyebrows were not quite as dark; they had blond highlights; and his eye lashes were lighter still. Rusty's complexion was unique. You've heard of peach fuzz—well, Rusty's skin was the peach and except for pits and pubes, his body hair was the fuzz. When I knew him, he had a rich suntan; but his skin didn't turn brown from the sun, it turned the color of a ripe peach. His ice blue eyes were startling, his nose was narrow and exquisitely shaped. His lips were thin and pale. He stood right at six feet tall and had an athletic frame, although he never showed much inclination for sports. Rusty was interested in computers and science. It's a shame things worked out for him the way they did. When I met him, he was doing time for burglary. If he'd had a normal childhood, he might have grown up to become one of the tops in the field of microtechnology. He was twenty-five when I got this story from him and he was teaching me things about computers that I hadn't learned, yet. You might even notice that he has a wider vocabulary and a better command of language than do most of the other guys in this book.

M Y MOTHER was a whore; I have no way of knowing who my father might have been. I'm certain that the only reason I didn't become an abortion statistic is that my mother wanted to be on welfare. The monthly checks continued to roll on in, whether she turned any tricks or not. The rent was paid, if nothing else, in order to be sure to have a place to conduct business.

I'm not being judgemental about prostitution, nor about having illegitimate children. I've personally known several bastards who grew up to be quite normal and functional. The bitterness you detect is the product of the perversions foisted on me by my mother. She would do anything for money (except work at an honest living, that is) and that included letting some of her tricks use me. I don't claim to understand why some men, ostensibly heterosexuals, would come to my mother and pay her for the use of her son's body. I left home before I ever got the chance to discuss this and other questions with my mother.

I was always big for my age; in school, I was always the biggest in my class. I've learned from experience that my unusual body tone (the color of my hair, the fleshiness of my muscles, the classical form of my bone structure, and the unique shade of bronze I acquire when I get a tan) is exciting to some. I've even had people tell me: "I'm not usually attracted to redheads, but you are a definite exception . . ." I was able to take advantage of that fact when I left home and had to fend for myself. But my mother also recognized this unique appeal, and quickly learned how to cash in on it. (Where do you think I learned? Is it appropriate to say, *at my mother's knee?*)

The first time is emblazoned in my memory. Unlike what child psychologists would have you think, it wasn't a traumatic experience. To the contrary, I thought the man in my bedroom was a nice man because he was one of the very few men who ever came to see my mother who paid me any attention. I was seven years old, but was wearing clothes designed for ten and eleven year olds. I had been asleep; my bedroom door opened, waking me up. My mother told the man to take as much time as he wanted. She left us alone; he sat on the edge of my bed and began talking to me. Within a very short time, his hands were under my pajama tops and he was tickling me.

I loved it! I thought it was great; I finally had someone to play with. He asked me if I liked being tickled, and I said yes. "All over?" he asked. Of course! What kid doesn't enjoy being tickled all over? I laughed so hard, my sides hurt. As he tickled me, he unbuttoned my pajama tops; then he tickled me lower and lower, until his hands were inside my shorts, beneath my pajama bottoms.

I thought nothing of it, because if you must know the truth, my mother used to feel my penis and play with it whenever she gave me a bath. And other times.

The man asked if he could come to bed with me, and I said sure. He made me watch him while he got naked, and he asked me what I thought about his grown up pee-pee.

Oh well, you get the idea. The guy was a real sicko, but in all truthfulness, we had a lot of fun that night. Over the years, there were other men; lots of them. Once in awhile, one of the men would hurt me; but usually, all I had to do was cry out and make him stop.

I knew that what was going on wasn't natural; but I was power-less to do anything about it until I reached puberty and began to get stronger and even bigger than I had been.

When I told my mother that I wasn't going to do it any more, she and I had a heated argument. I didn't leave home just then; I stuck around, hoping that we could work things out. However, instead of the tensions relaxing, the situation became more strained.

My mother's perversions took several twists over the years, in-cluding several forays into XXX-rated kiddy porn videos. (I'm sure some of those videos I starred in are still around, somewhere). When I was fourteen, even after we'd had our heated arguments, she met a man who was interested in using me in a video and she demanded that I participate, as I had been forced to do when I was younger. When I adamantly refused, she told me to get out. It was a vitriolic scene; she accused me of being a little ingrate who wanted to just lay around the house and do nothing while she sup-ported me! And so on.

I don't think she expected me to actually leave, because up till that time in my life, I had always been meek and subservient to her, never questioning her authority. However, I was growing up, and you can't keep kids in the dark forever. I was discovering for myself that I had a commodity which could be converted to cash, over and over again. I just didn't know where to go or how to get started.

I am a firm believer that a gay man is born that way; it is not a matter of choice or arbitrary decisions. Nor do I believe that I became gay simply because my mother allowed men to play with my body in my formative years. Homosexuality is not a perversion; it's as natural a phenomenon in the universe as any other variation of a species. In fact, I believe that the very lack of frequency of the variation makes it more precious, somehow more valuable, more beautiful. The rarer the species, the more delicate and precious it is in nature. Whenever I hear heterosexuals express hate or disgust for homosexuals, I am reminded of the fox and the sour grapes.

I didn't have much luck when I first hit the streets. I had only the vaguest idea about how to take care of myself. I knew there were men who would pay to have sex with me; I just didn't know how to find them. Like a lot of kids who run away from home, I discovered early that the opportunities present themselves almost immediately. While hitch-hiking out of town, hoping to get as far away from my mother as possible, I got my first offer. Having no money on me, I decided the time was ripe to get started.

Several tricks and numerous towns and cities later, I found myself in a large midwestern metropolis. I tried to rent a motel room with the money I'd made, but they wouldn't rent to a kid, even though I looked older than my fourteen years. I ended up sleeping under a bush near the railroad tracks. I awoke the next morning, cold and sore. I got a hot breakfast, then found plenty of time on my hands to go looking around. Nothing I did or saw that day helped me figure out how to get started in the prostitution business. Frankly, up till that time, the only thing I really knew about it was what I'd learned at home, and the operative word there is *home*. My mother had always worked out of her home; but I had no home, and no one would rent me one. So, I had to teach myself everything from scratch.

For the next few years, I managed to survive on the streets. I never became an expert at hustling, because my heart wasn't really in it; but I made enough to get by. I had a few hair-raising experiences, and once I was actually kidnapped when I was fifteen and held as a sex-slave by a perverted weirdo who kept me tied to a bed most of the time. Later, I managed to escape, but only after this creep committed suicide right in front of my eyes by blowing his brains out with a hand gun. I had thought he was going to kill me, too, but he didn't.

But not all of my experiences were bad. I learned how to suck cock like a pro and I learned how to take it up the ass, and I learned how to do whatever needed to be done to keep money in my pocket; but it wasn't a happy time for me. I dreamed about going back to school and maybe learning about computers and how to make video games, and so on. It just never worked out that way.

By the time I was eighteen, I had lost most of my drive and ambition. I had been homeless for years, and couldn't see anything better in my future. I've never even spent a single day in high school; so my chances of making a legitimate living in this fucked up old world were slim.

I spent a lot of time at rescue missions, suffering through the religious crap just to get a meal, which was nothing more than slop. The reason I ate at the missions was because I wasn't always in the mood for sex, and sex was the only way I knew how to make money. Sometimes, I just wanted to lie down and die, but that feeling never lasted too long. I'm a survivor, even if I'm not highly motivated.

I pretty much stayed in the Midwest during those years. Only later did I move out West, and that turned out to be a mistake, because I eventually wound up in prison. But that was a few years after this particular incident, which happened in a town I'd never been in previously.

Excuse me for being immodest for a moment, but I know I'm attractive enough to command a good price and I know there's a lot of men who are willing to pay to take me to bed; I'm even a damned good cock sucker, having learned when I was much younger. But that particular town just didn't seem to have much action going for it, and I couldn't find any tricks.

Having had no luck, I was walking aimlessly in a seedy part of town, when a pleasant sounding voice interrupted my thoughts. The guy started talking to me and told me that he had seen me at the mission. He told me his name was Ricky. We talked for awhile and I found out that he, too, had run away from home when he was a kid. Then he asked me if I was gay, or did I at least like to fuck around with other guys.

I didn't answer at first; so he rushed to explain his question. "I've done a lot of hustling, and I figure you have, too. Right now, though, I'm broke. I know how to come up with some money, but I need someone to do it with me."

"Do what?" I asked.

"There's this guy on the other side of town. He's got his own house, although it's nothing fancy. He likes guys, but he likes them two at a time. It's like this: he likes to watch two guys having sex together. I need someone who's willing to have sex with me while this guy watches."

"You don't even know me," I commented in astonishment. "What makes you think I'd be willing to have sex with you? And why would I want to put on a show for someone else?"

"For the money. We're both broke, right? It's easy money, because all we gotta do is have sex with each other, not with him. I'm not bad looking, am I? It could be fun."

Even though he was a year older than me, Ricky was the same height as me and approximately the same build, except that I was actually more muscular than he was. In fact, he looked a little undernourished. He looked like an average teenager, with a nose that was just a little bit too big and an adam's apple that highlighted his long neck. He was attractive in an average sort of way. By that I mean, he was definitely not a teen idol, but neither was he ugly or gangly. Our brief encounter immediately put me in the dominant situation, since he was begging me for a favor and since I was the more attractive of the two of us. (I know that sounds egotistical; but I don't mean for it to be. If I don't say it, how will the readers know?)

Ricky told me that he had to be sure that I would do it with him; otherwise, the guy wouldn't pay us. He wanted to test me, first. On our way across town, we found a place behind a billboard, in an area of light traffic. No one could see us unless they were to come directly upon us, and that was highly unlikely.

He explained that the guy we were going to see, Mylo, was confined to a wheelchair and was impotent. We wouldn't have to do anything with him, but when we got started with each other we would have to make it last about an hour or so. Anything less than that, Mylo would feel cheated and not want to pay us. While telling me this, Ricky undid the buttons on my jeans and fished around for my cock. He stroked it until it got hard, then he pulled it out and went down on his knees. He sucked on it for just about a minute, then got up. "So far, so good," he said. "Now do that to me."

When he saw me look at him funny, he hurried to explain that he was just making sure I wasn't going to fink out on him when we got there. So I pulled his cock out of his pants and sucked on it for a moment. "Satisfied?" I asked, standing up.

He said it was great. Then he thanked me profusely. He was stone broke and really needed the money. I asked him why it was so hard to find tricks in this town. He told me that there was no special area where hustlers went; no designated area for hanging out. I began to formulate a plan of my own, but I didn't tell him about it.

It seemed as though we walked forever, but we finally arrived in a residential neighborhood, where the houses were small and the yards didn't see a lot of meticulous care. Mylo's house was on a corner lot; the front yard was composed entirely of cement, with a few lawn ornaments set near the house. Ricky rang the bell at the front door and a moment later we were inside.

Ricky introduced us and asked him if he was in the mood for a show. He looked me over and then slowly nodded his head. Then he smiled and said, "By all means, young gentlemen. Go on into the living room. This is a delightful surprise. But why didn't you call first?"

Ricky told Mylo that he was so broke, he didn't even have the price of a phone call. I could have killed him! I wondered what would have happened if Mylo had already had a couple of kids over that night. The walk across town seemed like ten miles. I was really pissed, but I didn't want to piss Ricky off in front of Mylo; so I said nothing. We went inside.

The entry hall was made of hardwood flooring, as was most of the house, I learned later; but the sunken living room had wall to wall carpet. Mylo kept his house fairly dark. A lamp in one corner of the living room provided dim lighting and I could see that it was sparsely furnished: an over-stuffed chair, a two piece sectional couch, a coffee table, and a couple of end tables. The front wall was solid drapery; an unused fireplace occupied most of the side wall. It was obvious that Mylo rarely used this room.

He ushered us in and told us to have a seat, then he went down the hall into some other part of his home.

We removed our coats, threw them on the chair, then sat on different parts of the sectional. Ricky said that Mylo would be right back. He told me he was getting us a couple of Pepsis and a couple of twenty dollar bills. We would get the Pepsis right away; the money wouldn't come until we had finished with our show and had put our clothes back on and were ready to leave.

"Mylo's a Vietnam vet; got his legs shattered in the war. He carries a loaded gun in that wheelchair, just in case someone thinks about trying to take advantage of him."

He told me that Mylo never said much; that he usually just watched from the entry at the top of the steps leading down to the sunken room. "Just follow my lead, but do what you feel like doing, too. Don't hold back; he doesn't like it when it looks like you're not getting into it."

Mylo returned with the Pepsis and asked me lots of questions while we drank them. He then wheeled over to the area of the front door and flipped a switch. It turned on a light set near the ceiling in one of the front corners of the room. It was like a spot light, but angled away from the window so that we wouldn't cast silhouettes on the drapes.

When a lull developed in the conversation, Ricky stood up and moved the coffee table out of the center of the room, placing it near the fireplace. He then motioned for me to stand up. He took hold of my shoulders and pointed my body toward Mylo, then moved behind me. Seductively, he wrapped his arms around me and kissed me on the neck while slowly undoing the buttons of my shirt.

Even though I'd been having sex with men since I was seven, often in front of a video camera, I felt awkward and wooden at first. I was as self-conscious as a convict eating a wiener in front of his straight cellmate. But I knew I had to get into the swing of things; so I began to rotate my hips and grind them into his pelvis while he pulled my shirt open, leaving the ends just barely tucked into the waistband of my jeans. He feverishly ran his hands up and down over my chest and stomach, pausing at my tits to squeeze one and pinch the other.

The light from the corner highlighted our bodies by casting

shadows which created definition where none had previously existed. I tried to imagine what Mylo was seeing and I decided that the combination of light and shadow would have made a highly seductive visual effect.

I raised my arms and put my hands behind Ricky's head and threaded my fingers through his hair while pulling his head tightly into my neck, then I twisted my head and found his lips and engaged in a wet, sloppy, and feverish kiss.

From the entry hall, I heard a quietly murmured, "Very nice, very nice!"

My mother had taught me how to kiss like that—frantic and sloppy, with lips and tongue and teeth working passionately against the other person's mouth.

I caught Ricky by surprise, but he managed to follow my lead and while we appeared to be fighting over who was going to control whom during the course of the kiss, he pulled at the top buttons of my jeans and shoved his hand into my shorts, grabbing a fistful of hard cock.

I broke away from the kiss and turned to face him. While I unbuttoned his shirt, he slipped mine off my shoulders and pulled my arms out of the sleeves, then threw it on top of our jackets. While I finished removing his shirt, he stood in front of me gyrating his pelvis, like dancing in place. I realized that my body was blocking the view of Ricky's choreography from Mylo; so I sank to my knees while pulling the shirt off his arms. Holding the shirt sleeves, with the bulk of the shirt behind Ricky's butt, I pulled first the left, then the right sleeve, in time with Ricky's swinging hips.

Then I snapped the shirt away, which prompted Ricky to stop dancing and, still on my knees, I sucked at his cock through the denim material of his jeans. His hard tool was making a sizable bulge and it wasn't difficult to figure out where to blow hot air through the material.

I think we both realized simultaneously that we had better be careful or we wouldn't last an hour. We would either wear ourselves out physically, or we'd bust our nuts prematurely. Just as I was planning to pull away and reduce some of the heated passion I was beginning to feel, he put his hands on my head and nudged me away from his groin.

While still on my knees in front of him, I untied his shoe laces, but made no effort to remove the high-top sneakers he wore. He stretched his arms upward and outward, as if waking up and yawning. I figured he was doing that for Mylo's benefit, because even from the floor it looked wildly sexy to see his body stretched out, his muscles taut, and his stomach flat as a board. The light from the ceiling corner emphasized the depression in his solar plexus beneath his rib cage and exaggerated his muscles, which the stretch and yawn made look bigger and more developed.

I lifted my arms and slid my hands up along his naked stomach, so flat now that it felt hard and firm beneath my fingers. He relaxed his stretching as my hands ran up his chest, then glided back down along his sides, circling behind him and coming to a stop on the coarse material of his jeans covering his buttocks.

I thought about pulling off his pants, but then reminded myself that it was still early in the evening; so I rose to my feet and turned again to face Mylo, pressing my butt into Ricky's groin.

He lowered his arms and wrapped them around my midsection. My jeans had slipped down a little, but my hips are wide enough to hold them up unless all the buttons are undone. I've seen videos of myself and I know that the white waistband of my shorts creates a striking contrast against the bronze of my flesh when I've got a nice tan. I had to imagine that, under the scrutiny of that spotlight in the corner, the effect was not lost on Mylo.

I don't think I'm capable of describing every tiny detail of what went on during the time Ricky and I were putting on that show for Mylo, and even if I did it would do nothing more than drag out this story unnecessarily; so I'm going to compress the action. You'll simply have to take my word for it that we put on one hell of a show for Mylo and that he was more than satisfied by the time we were done.

It was interesting that I was getting a look at Ricky's naked body for the first time, each time I took something off him. I had imagined him with a smaller, less filled-out body than what came to light as his clothes came off. I believe I was enjoying our sex play as much as Mylo was. Until that night in Mylo's house, my only sex partners had been mature men, usually in their forties and fifties. Ricky was the first guy my own age, or thereabouts, that I had sex with, and I was loving every minute of it.

Ever so slowly, but with what I hoped was tantalizing sexuality, we took each other's clothes off—shoes, socks, pants. When we were reduced to nothing but boxer shorts for him and jockey briefs for me, we did a lot of reaching into and holding on, making sure that Mylo could see the sizable bulges beneath the white cotton material. Ricky's cock frequently poked through the slit in his shorts, while mine merely strained against the knitted cotton briefs. At all times during the hour or so that we played with each other, felt each other, sucked on each other, I think I was more conscious than Ricky of the lighting and its effects on what Mylo was treated to visually.

When I decided to take my shorts off, I had my back to Mylo and I whispered to Ricky to pull my shorts down slowly. I wanted Mylo to be treated to the sight of my buns slowly being revealed. Ricky managed to drag it out and to make it seductive as hell. When he pulled them from around my feet, he stood up and we embraced for awhile, kissing and rubbing bodies, all the time my back was to Mylo. He hadn't yet seen my cock.

I then began to walk backward, pulling Ricky with me, getting closer to Mylo. When the heels of my feet touched the step leading up from the living room to the entry hall, I knew that less than eighteen inches stood between us and Mylo. I then sank to my knees, pulling Ricky's boxers off him at the same time. Now we were both completely naked, and I turned to face Mylo. I could tell by the look on his face that he was pleased with our performance, and I know that he wished he had been capable of joining us.

I took Ricky by the hand and led him up the two steps to the landing. We stood next to Mylo's wheelchair, one of us on each side. I made sure that my cock pressed against Mylo's arm. There was nothing wrong with the top half of the vet's body. In fact, up close, I could see that he had a well-defined chest and that his biceps appeared to have been the product of conscientious efforts at strengthening and building. Mylo was not unattractive. I was glad I had brought him directly into our sex play, because it made me realize that he wasn't just some perverted freak in a wheelchair wishing he could get his nuts off while two teenage boys played with each other. He was a feeling human being, a man who suffered through no fault of his own.

I leaned across Mylo's body and kissed Ricky, pressing my cock ever more firmly against Mylo's arm. While we lingered in our kiss, Mylo took the opportunity to grip both of our cocks; he stroked them for us while we felt each other up across the space between us.

After a moment of playing with our cocks, Mylo's hands slipped around behind us and he lovingly felt our buns and as much of our bodies as he could reach. I didn't know if any of the other kids who put on shows for Mylo had thought to bring him into it, but probably not. Kids my age are usually very selfish and self-centered. They usually want to get their money and get the hell out of Dodge. One of the things I had learned at my mother's knee was that it was always important to make sure the customer was happy. Good old mom (I say sarcastically); she taught me a couple of things which I still feel are important.

After allowing Mylo to fondle our dicks, our buns, our nuts and whatever else he felt like, I led Ricky back to the living room and into the spotlight. We felt each other's body, we sucked each other's dick, and we played with each other for quite a while, roaming around the living room, flopping on the couch, spreading out on the floor, and generally having a good time with each other in as many positions as we could think of. We never actually fucked each other, but several times we pretended to, humping each other between the legs or from an angle where you couldn't tell what was going on. The only reason I wouldn't let Ricky fuck me was that there was no Vaseline or K-Y jelly.

I took a wild guess as to the time, since neither of us had a watch and there was no clock in the room; but when I felt certain the hour was up, I crawled between Ricky's legs in the middle of the floor. His body was pointed away from Mylo—his head closer to the steps and his feet closer to the fireplace. I sucked on Ricky's cock while he thrashed around, moving his legs and arms like an insect caught in a spider's web, struggling to get free. I didn't turn loose of his cock until his body convulsed in a hectic orgasm. I loved the feel of his cock shooting its hot sperm into my mouth. It was so thick and rigid; the loads of cum were prefaced by spurting sensations along the length of his iron hard tool. And I loved the way his body bucked beneath me, like a bronc trying to throw its rider.

When at last, his body slumped into a calm repose, the last of the convulsions and contractions having sent one final load of hot cum into my throat, I continued to lick his genitals. Several times, he shivered when my tongue pressed a sensitive spot.

When I finally got to my feet, he was exhausted. Nonetheless, he now got up with me and I again led him over to the wheelchair. This time, I stood directly in front of Mylo, my hard cock jutting straight out in front of me like the arm of a beefy gladiator rendering a salute to Caesar. Ricky stood behind me, remaining on the first step, while I stood on the next step up, gripping my cock in my hand and beginning a slow stroking and pumping. I couldn't be sure how Mylo would react to the idea of a grand finale consisting of me masturbating in front of him and shooting my wad into his lap. It might piss him off to get cum all over him; or it might trip his trigger. I decided to play it by ear.

With Ricky behind me, his hands running up and down my body, between my legs, over my tits, and generally making me feel good all over, I accelerated my pumping and my humping. I looked into Mylo's eyes and saw that he was pleased with my performance. He smiled an encouragement to continue. I did.

After an hour of hot sex play, I was ready to bust a nut with a shattering climax. Mylo was leaning forward in his wheelchair, almost doubled over, as if trying to reach his mouth out to touch my thick, swollen meat. I pounded away at my dick and felt the tingling sensation of orgasm shooting into every part of my body. My face became hot and my eyes squinted uncontrollably, while my body shuddered, then felt as though it was going to explode.

I stepped up to the entry landing, even with Mylo's wheelchair. His mouth could almost touch my cock, and I almost thrust it forward to let him suck me off, but it was too late for that. The sperm surged through my nuts and into my cock, just as my torso jerked forward. Suddenly, a long stringy rope of cum erupted from the head of my cock and shot toward Mylo's face. I saw the look of surprise as it whipped out and splattered on his nose and lips. He opened his mouth wide and tried to catch as much of it as possible, but some of it merely sprayed his face.

I erupted a second time, but the ejaculation was not as explosive as the first wad, and it merely landed in his lap; but he didn't seem to mind at all. In fact, judging from the look on his face, he was in seventh heaven. He reached for my dick and helped me finish the orgasm which had nearly buckled my knees. Luckily, Ricky had stayed behind me and had balanced me when my body was jerking so violently.

Mylo milked the last of the cum from my nuts through my fuck shoot and smeared it all around. When the last convulsion of my orgasm shuddered through my body, I sank to my knees. He licked his fingers and wiped the cum from his face, then licked his fingers again.

The evening had been a big success, and Mylo didn't hold back his praise. He had been relatively quiet through the whole thing, but now he raved about how great we had been. He brought us another Pepsi and paid us our money. While talking to him, I asked if he would allow us to use his shower to clean up.

He told me bluntly that he didn't usually let anyone into his house beyond the living room; but he had been so pleased with what we had done, he decided to allow it. (That's when I learned that the rest of the house had hardwood flooring and was built for the handicapped. Even the bathroom was designed for a paraplegic.)

He invited us back, but insisted that we call first, if at all possible. He lived on a limited income and didn't always have the money to afford to pay for a show.

On the way back to the downtown area, I asked Ricky to show me how to find a gay bar. He knew where several were; which one did I have in mind? I told him that I wanted one where the customers could see me hitchhiking when they left.

To make a long story short, I had decided to try to set up a little red-light district for male hustlers. I wasn't sure if it would catch on, but I knew it was something that was needed in a town that size.

Across the street from one of the local gay bars, I hung out until I got a ride with someone leaving the bar. That night was spent in a warm bed; and most other nights, as well.

My idea paid off, and soon afterwards, Ricky and I were joined by other kids with hot young bodies for sale.

That was seven years ago; but to the best of my knowledge, the Vaseline Alley which I personally created is still going strong.

ROBBY AND THE
SUBURBAN TRADE

When describing one of my characters, I don't like to use movie stars as comparisons. A writer should use the tools of his craft to create mental images for his readers. However, in Robby's case, I can't resist telling my readers that he strongly resembles Corey Haim, the kid with the laboratory research dog in the Dean Koontz movie, The Watchers. *Robby has those same delicate, fine features and that same little boyish quality. Robby's body is as slight of frame and as supple in muscular structure as the young movie star I've referred to. He has the same cupid's bow shape for lips and the same cute little button of a nose. The eyebrows come to a pixie-like point over soft blue eyes with blond lashes. To watch him step wringing wet from a shower is to understand why he was in such great demand in the suburbs.*

WHEN I was growing up, my closest friend was a guy named Jerry, who I met in the second grade. It's not strange that we became such good friends, because we had a lot in common. Both of us came from poor parents, and in my case I never even knew my father, while Jerry's father and mother got divorced just before we became close friends. We both had a younger brother, and it seemed like we never had any of the great toys and games that the other kids in school had. Our mothers had it pretty tough, raising kids without a man around to help out with the finances.

When we were teenagers, though, it seemed like Jerry was always coming up with spending money. He always had money for the video arcades and the movies and cokes and candies and things. At first, he told me he had a part time job, and I believed him, because there was lots of nights when he got lost and I couldn't find him. I asked him if he could get me a part time job, too, but he just told me that there wasn't enough work to go around. I kept trying to find a part time job on my own, but the most I could ever come up with was mowing lawns or washing cars and stuff like that. A teenager always needs pocket money and I just never seemed to have any. Jerry always had plenty of money for both of us.

I begged and begged him to fill me in on what he was doing to earn so much money. One day, he made me promise to keep everything he told me an absolute secret. When I agreed, he told me that one day he had been hitch-hiking and got picked up by a guy who offered him money just to feel his *thing*. Jerry had never been shy or bashful; so he let the guy go ahead and play with his dick until he had jacked him completely off. After that, it happened more often, with lots of different guys. After awhile, he found out that he could hitch-hike along a particular county road and always count on making some money.

He told me that the going rate was five dollars if all they did was jack him off; ten dollars if he had to give them the hand-job; and twenty dollars if he gave them a blow job.

I looked at him like he was crazy. I couldn't believe that he gave blow jobs! He told me there was nothing to it. At first, it was sorta strange, but after that, you got used to it, and it wasn't bad at all. It sure was easy to make twenty bucks real fast.

So that was how he was doing it! I asked him if I could do the same thing, but without giving blow jobs. He said sure; but after awhile, he said, I'd want to make more money and I'd end up giving blow jobs, too.

I didn't think so, at the time; but I was anxious to make some money, even if it meant jacking off some guy in his car, or getting jacked off myself. Jerry told me that I had to wear a T-shirt, loose fitting jeans and no underwear, and on warm afternoons and evenings, it was even best to take off your shirt and slip it through a loop in your jeans on the left side. The T-shirt looped through the jeans had become a well-known sign of availability along that road, which was the main connecting link between the downtown area, and the richest suburb in the county: lots of million dollar homes and sprawling estates. Don't get me wrong, though; not everyone who picked us up was a rich guy. I only made five dollars my first time out.

Jerry went along with me my first time, making sure that I was dressed (or maybe *undressed*) properly. I wore no shorts and I tucked my T-shirt through a loop in my jeans. Jerry had coached me for several days leading up to that Saturday afternoon. He told me what to expect if the ride wanted some action and what to do if the driver turned out to be a "rube." When we got to the pickup spot, he bitched that my jeans weren't loose enough. It was the loosest pair I had, I told him; so he made me undo the top button and even made me ease the zipper down about an inch. I felt totally naked, standing there, but he assured me it was the best way to make sure I made some money.

He hid behind a nearby billboard and I stuck out my thumb to hitch a ride. Within two minutes, I got picked up by a guy in an older model car. It surprised me how young he was: only about thirty or so, and not bad looking, except for looking like a nerd, with horn rim glasses and white shirt and tie. When he asked how far I was going, I told him, "Just down the road."

I was a new face on the circuit (as Jerry called it), but even though he was nervous, it didn't take him long to get around to asking me if I wanted to make a few bucks. "Sure," I told him with a bright smile, like Jerry told me to do. Then he asked me if I knew what he wanted, and I said yes, "Sort of."

He asked me what I meant by that, and I told him it depended on how much he was willing to pay. When he told me he only had five bucks on him, I figured he knew just what that much money would buy. Jerry told me to always make sure that we were in agreement; so I asked him if he wanted to give me a hand job. He said, yeah, and pulled a five dollar bill out of his shirt pocket, reached over and slipped it into my jeans, right at the zipper.

At that point, I started to get a little nervous. I wasn't sure if I could go through with it. I had never done anything like that before and even though it had been easy to talk about it with Jerry, I discovered that I was getting butterflies at the thought of this total stranger jacking me off.

His car had bucket seats and when he reached over and put the money into my jeans, I realized he would have to pull over somewhere to do it, because if he did it while he was driving, he'd kill us both. Jerry had told me that it was okay to stop some place, because there was lots of places to park along the county road where we could do our thing without being seen. He told me not to let the guy take me very far off the road, and that if he did, I should jump and run at the first chance I got. He said that there was hardly ever anything to worry about; but just be careful.

The "circuit" section of the county road was lined with fruit orchards for about ten miles. Every mile or so, there was a deserted fruit stand which usually did big business during the harvest seasons. The driver pulled off the roadway and drove into a prune orchard. The prunes were still green plums; so no one would be working that field for several more months. The driver told me he was sure that no one would discover us.

When he stopped the car and killed the engine, he reached over nervously and unzipped my zipper all the way down. (I had already pocketed the five dollar bill). He talked to me while he reached in and took hold of my cock, which was starting to get hard.

He told me he hadn't seen me before and wondered if I was new on the circuit. I told him I was, but quickly added that I had a friend who was looking out for me.

He saw that I was nervous and a little scared; so he told me not to worry, he would never try to hurt me. He said that, as far as he knew, no kid had ever been harmed on the circuit.

While he talked, he unzipped his own pants and pulled out his own dick and started stroking himself with his left hand while he was fondling me with his right one. "God, you're nice," he said, feeling my smooth chest and flat stomach, then reaching again for my cock.

His grip was firm and pleasant and even without my shirt I felt hot. But I didn't think he was going to be able to get me off because his grip just didn't excite me. Whenever I jack myself off, I whip it real fast and concentrate on a spot just beneath the helmet. When I'm ready to shoot my wad, I wrap my whole palm around the head of my dick and let it squirt. This guy was holding my cock tightly enough, but he wasn't concentrating on the head and he wasn't going fast enough.

I felt funny, just sitting there, letting him jack me off; but I figured I would probably get used to it. It was an easy way to make five bucks.

When he told me to pull my pants all the way down, I felt uncomfortable; but Jerry had prepared me for that. He told me never to take them all the way off, but it was okay to pull them down to my knees or ankles. So I did what he said and for awhile he just fondled my nuts and my legs. It felt good, but I was starting to go soft and when he noticed it, he started stroking me again.

By now he was pumping his own cock pretty fast. I told him to stroke me off just as fast, if he wanted me to cum.

But it was too late. All of a sudden, he started twisting and jerking and I could see him shooting jism all over his hand. He felt my stomach and chest, then held onto my nuts while he was cumming. He moaned loudly, saying things like "Oh that's great! Oh wow! Oh, God, you're nice," and so on.

After a minute or so, he let go of me and reached under his seat and brought out a towel with which he wiped himself off. He sat there breathing heavy for a few minutes, still feeling my body, but no longer playing with my cock.

Then he pulled his hand away and started the engine. "We'd better get out of here," he said, like a burglar who had been in a house too long. "Better pull your pants up."

Jerry had told me that there would be times when it would happen that way. Some guys just want to feel you up while they jack themselves off. He told me not to worry; there would be lots of chances to get a nut when working the circuit, and it was best to hold off, because sometimes you'd get worn out in the first half hour.

"If you shoot your wad three times in the first hour, then can't get it hard, you can't make any more money," he had told me. "Better not to catch a nut, if you can help it."

I pulled up my pants while the driver headed back to the road. He let me off and I crossed to the other side and stuck out my thumb.

My second ride wanted me to jack him off while he drove around. He gave me a ten dollar bill and I moved over on the seat closer to him. He was an older man in his fifties, but he was real nice and even a little bit fatherly. It didn't take him long to catch a nut. He, too, had a towel under the front seat, and he told me to wipe him and myself with it.

"You do that pretty good, young fella," he said when he dropped me off.

"Thanks," I said. The only thing I could think of was that I did it to him like I usually did to myself.

I had made fifteen bucks, and was feeling pretty good; but I didn't want to turn any more tricks just yet; I wanted to talk to Jerry. So I walked back to our meeting place near the big billboard and waited for him to show up.

I only had to wait about ten minutes. He caught me by surprise when he poked his head around the billboard posts and asked me how I did.

"So far, so good," he said. Then he took out two twenty dollar bills and waved them at me. "I did pretty good, too!"

That forty dollars looked so much better than my fifteen; but I knew he'd had to suck a couple of dicks to get it. "How do you stand it?" I asked. "I just can't imagine letting some guy shoot his jism into my mouth!"

"It's easy," he told me. "If the guy's cum tastes bitter, I try to spit it out on the towel which is usually hidden under the front seat. If it's not sour, then it actually tastes pretty good. You'll see. Someday."

He wanted to quit for the day, but I wanted to make at least five or ten bucks more; so I told him I'd meet him at the arcade later and he split.

It was starting to get cool, but I didn't want to put on my T-shirt. I didn't want any misunderstandings: I was ready to turn some tricks! I guess you could say I was already starting to get greedy. A good hustler has to be a little bit greedy or he'll never make it.

I got two more rides before joining Jerry at the arcade and had made ten bucks on each of them. One guy offered me twenty for a blow job, but I couldn't bring myself to do it, not just yet.

We did it every night for a week, and I really perked up at the money I was making. I was beginning to wish I had gotten started at thirteen, like Jerry.

After a week of riding the circuit, Jerry and I were having a pizza and he said to me, "Now that you've got your dick wet, how'd you like to make some *real* money?"

It turns out that he knew several gay couples in the suburbs who paid a lot more. "Fifty, sometimes even a hundred bucks. Usually, you gotta spend the night if they pay you a hundred."

"A hundred?" I couldn't believe it. A hundred bucks, just to have sex with some guy over night. "Hell yes," I told him enthusiastically.

"We gotta tell our folks that we're going camping or something, otherwise they'll wonder where we are."

I told him that my mom already thought I was spending too much time mowing lawns and weeding gardens, but she was glad that I was able to make some spending money. "If my mom knew what I was doing, she'd kill me!"

"Mine, too," Jerry said. "But I never let her see how much money I've got. But what do you say? This Friday night?"

It was agreed that I would break into the overnight trade, and Jerry even made a date with a couple in the rich suburb: Ralph and Mark.

On Friday afternoon, we met at the billboard and worked the circuit all the way out to the suburbs. I picked up three ten dollar rides. We met at a predetermined spot and waited for about half an hour until Mark came by in his brand new Cadillac to pick us up.

Mark was a strikingly handsome man in his mid to late thirties. He was a doctor with a private practice. Ralph was a computer analyst, or something like that. Their home was like a fucking mansion! It was on a private road on the side of a small hill, overlooking a vineyard. There were only a couple of other homes on that road, and they were so far apart that privacy would never be a problem.

Ralph wasn't as handsome as Mark, and he had a little bit of a beer belly, but he wasn't bad looking. I guess I was expecting a gay couple to be weirdos or fruitcakes or something. Turns out they were both real nice guys. I don't think you'd know they were gay if you passed them on the streets or met them at a party. I mean, except for the fact that they were both men, they were just an ordinary couple who made good money.

Ralph had made dinner (Caesar salad, steaks and truffles, and baked potato with all the fixings). We had wine with dinner, but they gave me and Jerry small glasses and told us to sip it. They didn't want us getting drunk.

The sun was going down when all four of us stripped naked and went skinny dipping in their humungous pool. There was a lot of touching and feeling and groping, but no serious sex play for awhile.

Both of them had taken Jerry to bed lots of times in the past;

so I was the new guy and they both fawned over me, making me feel special. It was kind of strange to have two men after my body at the same time.

After drying off and going back inside, we all stayed nude. The house was dimly lit and soft rock music came out of nowhere. It was neat, just lying around naked, being felt up by Ralph and Mark practically every minute. I mean, you couldn't even move without someone copping a feel of your dick or your buns or your nuts or your chest. I'm not bitching, though; it felt pretty good, and it was a totally new experience for me.

The large, step-down living room was covered with a thick piled carpet and the furniture was plush and covered with rich fabrics. A large screen TV sat near the stone work fireplace and one of the most expensive stereos I've ever seen filled at least half the length of one of the walls. Luxurious drapes, partially opened, covered the sliding glass windows which opened onto the back yard, where the pool we had swam in took up only a small part of the open area. In addition to the pool, there was a spacious lawn, some trees, shrubs, and a concrete patio between the living room and what looked like a small house, which I later learned was a sauna, complete with shower and change room. Growing up poor, I had never seen such a magnificent house!

They offered us watered down cocktails and at that point, Mark paired off with me and Ralph paired off with Jerry. Mark made me finish my drink, then he wrapped his powerful arms around me and embraced me, holding me close to him and rubbing our crotches together. He treated me gently, like I imagined you would treat a girl. His hands caressed my bare shoulders and glided down my smooth back to my buns. I'll be honest with you: I had never been felt up like that before, and it was a totally wild experience.

On the floor, Ralph was lying on top of Jerry, kissing him and feeling him up. This was all so strange to me and I didn't know what to do except go along with the program. I just let Mark do whatever he felt like doing.

After a few moments of quiet intimacy, Mark whispered in my ear, "Come with me, I've got something special for you." He took me by the hand and led me out of the living room and into the kitchen where he took a can of spray whipped cream and some fresh strawberries from the fridge. "You'll enjoy this," he promised as he led me down the hallway into one of the bedrooms.

A round bed filled most of the room, even though the room was pretty large for a bedroom.

He told me to lie down while he shook the spray can vigorously. When I was in the middle of the bed, he crawled on and began spraying whipped cream on me, first down my neck to my chest, then circling each of my nipples, then down to my belly button where he created a sundae-like peak, then continued to spray down to my genitals. He created another peak on my now erect dick. He threw the can on the floor and picked up the basket of strawberries and popped one of them into my mouth and ate one himself. Then he put one on each of my nipples, one on the peak at my belly button, and one on the peak at my dick. The berry tasted delicious and I knew Mark was going to enjoy his little treat, almost as much as I was going to.

I enjoyed it even more than I thought I would. It was *wild*. His tongue licked off the cream slowly, while his fingers tried to find all of my erogenous zones (although I didn't know then that they were called that). He licked down to my left nipple, then sucked the berry into his mouth. He then kissed me and squished the berry while our lips were joined. The sweet juice dripped onto my tongue and down my throat. After a lingering kiss, he did the same with the berry on my right nipple. Then he licked his way down my body to the strawberry on my navel. He again shared the berry with me, then sucked the whipped cream away from my navel with such powerful suction that I thought he was going to suck it right out of me.

I lay there and enjoyed what he was doing. When he sucked and licked the whipped cream off my dick, it was maddening because he never really applied very much pressure until after it was all licked off. But I think the wildest sensation came when he sucked my balls. He stroked my dick with wet fingers while he popped each of my testicles into his mouth and rolled them around with his tongue. I couldn't believe this guy was going to pay me a hundred dollars for the pleasure of bringing me so much pleasure!

When he finished licking everything off, he climbed on top of me and lay there for a few minutes, rubbing our naked, sticky bodies together. When he rolled off of me, he said, "Your turn."

"I've never done anything like that before," I said lamely.

"I just taught you everything you need to know," he said with a smile. "Now do the same to me. That's what I'm paying you for."

I wished he hadn't said that. I was just having fun, and I didn't really want to think of myself like a whore or something. When you boil it all down, that's exactly what I was, but I hadn't thought about it that way until he told me he was paying me to do it to him. I remember losing my hardon when he said those words, but I don't think he noticed because I immediately started spraying whipped cream on him the same places he had done it to me.

I imitated all of his movements and actions, including squishing the berries into his mouth and even trying to suck his belly-button out of his body. He appeared to be enjoying himself thoroughly, and my hardon even came back by the time I got to his dick and his nuts.

His body was a lot hairier than mine, probably because he had twenty years on me; but it wasn't so hairy that I kept getting little hairs in my mouth. That only happened when I was sucking his balls. They were a lot bigger than mine, so I had to really work at trying to get both of them into my mouth at one time, but I eventually managed and I heard him moan with delight.

When I had finished licking up all the cream, I lay on top of him like he had done. I heard him moan, "Ooh, you learn fast, kid! That was great!"

He tumbled around with me for a little bit, then just rolled off the bed and said, "Come on, Robby. Let's do the sauna."

He left the whipped cream can and the berries in the bedroom and again led me by the hand through the house to the living room. Ralph and Jerry were nowhere in sight. Mark led me through the sliding glass door onto the cement patio.

Night had fallen and the only lights in the back yard were the ones in the pool and the light over the door to the sauna.

The sauna building was as big as a two-car garage. The door opened into a room with benches and hooks on the wall. This was the change room. One of the walls was lined with shelves and filled with towels of all sorts of colors. The door to the next room was on the far left. It led to the shower area, which glistened with white ceramic tiles, speckled with gold flakes. There were four shower heads and even fully tiled benches to sit on. Turning right, we walked through the shower and through another door. This one opened into the sauna itself.

The room was easily ten feet by twelve feet, with blond oak wood paneling on the ceiling and walls and solid oak planks providing two tiers of benches on three walls. Jerry was sprawled out on the top bench to my left and Ralph was crouched between his legs giving him a blow job. Both of them were totally naked and hadn't even brought any towels; but then, neither had me and Mark.

The hot air sucked away my breath; but within a few seconds, I was used to the dry heat and began to feel the perspiration forming all over my body. Mark poured something over the hot rocks in the center of the room, reached for a funny looking little bottle near Jerry's head, then sat beside me on the top tier of the right wall. We watched Ralph suck on Jerry's dick for a few minutes while the heat built up and our bodies developed rivers of running sweat. Mark unscrewed the lid of the little bottle and sniffed the contents.

"Butyl nitrate," he said in answer to my unspoken question. "Sometimes called *poppers*. Try it. It'll give you a rush. It's harmless and it'll make you feel great!"

I sniffed the bottle and felt a surge of heat cross over my face. It was incredible! I suddenly felt sexier than I had ever felt in my life! Mark toyed with my cock while we enjoyed the heat. I had to admit to myself that I was enjoying watching the action on the other side of the sauna, especially under the influence of the butyl nitrate.

I had never really taken a good close look at Jerry's body until then, when it was sprawled out on that sauna bench. He really had a nice physique: muscular arms and chest, flat but fleshy stomach, and slender (but not skinny) legs. Each time Ralph moved his mouth up along Jerry's cock, I could see that Jerry had been endowed with a healthy piece of meat. It was thick and swollen and long and Ralph seemed to be enjoying every inch of it.

The next thing I knew, Mark had swung himself off the bench and was kneeling between my thighs. My body was practically hairless and the sweat rolling off of me made my skin feel silky to the touch. Mark's hands glided along my thighs, touching every ticklish and hot spot on my legs. He stretched out his arms and felt up my stomach and chest, then reached for the poppers again.

"Take a hit at the very instant I go down on you," he said through glassy eyes.

Just as his thick, fleshy lips wrapped around the head of my dick, I sniffed the butyl nitrate and got such a rush—it was fantastic! My face exploded with the chemical rush and the head of my dick tingled with a new sensation. When Mark began a long, slow descent down the length of my shaft, I could feel every little bump on the surface of his tongue and every contour of my own cock. I squirmed with the pleasure of it all and swore to God I was going to melt into the woodwork. My body was hot and excited, tingling all over in places I didn't even know felt good.

I looked over at Jerry and saw him bent at the waist, pumping his cock into Ralph's mouth with a furious passion. His arms stretched out to Ralph's shoulders and his fingers looked like they were digging into Ralph's flesh, but Ralph didn't seem to mind—his mouth accepted the bucking thrusts from Jerry's dick and his face looked as though it was in heaven. Jerry's tightened stomach made a mountainous ridge stretching from his breast bone down to his groin, with little hollows on each side. Right then and there, I knew that one of these days, I was going to take Jerry to bed with me. I wanted his hot body. I wanted to feel his nips get hard while I was sucking on his thick hunk of fuckmeat. I also discovered, at that moment, that I liked smooth, hairless bodies. Ralph was nearly hairless and the two of them looked great together. Mark had the nicer body of the two men that Jerry and I were servicing that night, but his hairy chest and stomach didn't excite me the way Jerry's and Ralph's bodies did.

Over the years, I've found that, when it comes to either long-lasting relationships or just plain old hot and heavy sexual enjoyment, it doesn't really make much difference—hairy or smooth, it all depends on the person, not on his physical characteristics. But that night in the sauna, the slick and slippery smoothness of their bodies, dripping wet and glistening in the dim light of the sauna, turned me on while I watched. Jerry's shiny smooth body, with his hairless chest and silky smooth legs, looked so inviting while he fucked Ralph's face.

I could tell that Jerry was getting real close to hitting his peak because he was groaning and moaning like a mad man and his pelvis was slamming into Ralph's face with a rapid pounding that could only be signalling the onset of orgasm. That fleshy ridge of muscles running up along his stomach jerked and contracted and forced Jerry's upper body to hunch over to the point where his head almost touched Ralph's.

I took another sniff of the butyl nitrate just as Jerry exploded into Ralph's mouth and the effect was physically shattering! My face felt like it was on fire and I felt sexy as hell all over my body. Watching my best friend since childhood having sex with another man, their slippery bodies thrashing and squirming all over the top bench of the sauna, while yet another man was slurping away on my own cock between my legs, was such a scene of total pleasure and such a visual turn on that, mingled with the poppers, I was ready to cum without very much more coaxing from Mark. Greedily, I sniffed the bottle again and felt myself hurrying to my own orgasm.

Mark must have felt it coming, too, because he began to suck harder and faster, his hands gliding all over my wet, smooth body, down my thighs and calves and back up to my nuts and then on to my stomach and chest and arms, which had been hanging limp by my side until then. Now, I copied Jerry and placed my hands behind Mark's head, feeling the silky curls of his permed hair. His hands, now with more feverish intensity, glided more rapidly over my naked body, feeling and rubbing, sometimes hard, sometimes soft.

Then, just as I was ready to explode, I felt his finger toying with the muscles of my ass, which puckered uncontrollably at the gentle prodding of his finger. He didn't slip it all the way in, but the threat or the promise to do so sent new tingles of excitement into the head of my dick and I jerked uncontrollably, crashing over the top of the wave of orgasm, like a surfer wiping out after a righteous ride along the curl of a tsunami wave. Right at that point, Mark went all the way down on me, his hot wet lips completely encircling my dick, and he sucked with the pressure of a vacuum cleaner. My body jerked even more ferociously than Jerry's had done and I thought the convulsion was going to make me pull out of Mark's mouth, but his grip and suction were so tight that they merely urged me on to squirt even more and more cum into his hot mouth.

I felt the hot cum spurting through the tube inside my cock and could even imagine it hit the back of Mark's throat as it fired out unseen, followed by yet another. It was my first blow job and jacking off couldn't even begin to compare to it for pure thrill and excitement. I always liked feeling my own body when I jacked off, but getting a blow job meant that someone else was doing all the work and I was having all the pleasure.

Just as Mark was sucking the last of my sperm squirts out of my nuts, I looked over at Jerry and saw that he and Ralph had gotten wrapped up in watching me and Mark, just as we had watched them a few minutes earlier. Both of them were sitting up-right and Jerry had his hand in Ralph's crotch, holding his prick and slowly stroking it. I could tell that Jerry had done this a lot, and I wondered for a split second why he waited so long to bring me into this hidden world of his. I know he had been selling his body for at least two years. Maybe he had been afraid of how I would have reacted when I was younger. As close as we were, we had never talked about sex, except as school kids do—you know, mostly all those lies about liking this babe or that chick, and so on.

Our eyes connected and he winked at me, as if we were finally sharing super private secrets.

When Mark had sucked the last drop of cum out of my squirt-gun, my body went totally limp, like a man who collapses after running a marathon or something. For a long time, Mark just sucked on my dick, until it went totally soft, then he got up and sat beside me. The four of us talked for awhile, getting to know each other, except that Jerry had warned me to never tell the truth about my family and background—always make up stories, he told me, that way no one can ever come looking for you. Keep your real life a secret. Over the years, I learned the many reasons for doing what he said, but I had to admit that it was hard for me to make up stories without tripping over my own lies. To this day, I don't like telling lies, even though it's sometimes a neces-sary evil.

After awhile, we showered, then took another dip in the pool.

It was a warm evening, but it was starting to get a little cool; so we went inside and watched some videos on their VCR, including one X-rated gay video with a lot of real good looking surfer types. Later, we had another drink; this one a hell of a lot stronger than before, even though Mark insisted he didn't want to get us drunk.

That night, I slept with Ralph and Jerry slept with Mark. When we were in the bathroom, brushing our teeth, getting ready for bed, Jerry warned me that I would learn how to fuck that night. He told me that I didn't have to do it—I didn't have to do anything I didn't want to—but that if I wimped out, I'd screw myself out of half of the money. In other words, part of what was expected for the hundred bucks they were paying each of us was that they could fuck us. I can't say I enjoyed it, but when it happened, I just tried to pretend like I did. Ralph was gentle and he used Vaseline to make his cock slip in easy without causing any pain. But I've never gotten used to being fucked. I guess I'm strictly oral, when it comes to sex.

After that, Jerry introduced me to several different guys, singles and couples, spread out all over the suburbs. There was never any problem about competing with each other, because there were always more customers than we could handle. Believe it or not, my favorite became an older man in his late fifties.

The old guy was a lot richer than Mark and Ralph put together, and his place was like a fucking palace; but he was alone. All alone and apparently quite lonely. He enjoyed having me drop by, even if we didn't have sex. He liked talking some, and I enjoyed listening to him. He was some bigshot corporate executive in the semi-conductor business who kept his love life a secret. He told me that I had become the lover he had always wanted but had never found time for, and it didn't matter that he had to pay me for it, he was just glad he could help me out financially. He really was a pretty swell guy! After awhile, he started giving me a hundred bucks every time I came by, even if it was just for an hour or two or even just to talk.

I miss those times in the suburbs, but it was fun while it lasted, and the money was good. I continued to work the circuit and the suburbs after high school and supported myself through college by turning tricks. After college, I got out of the business; but every

now and then I go back and see some of my former customers.
If we have sex these days, it's not for money but strictly for the
fun and pleasure of it.

AIDS RISK REDUCTION GUIDELINES
FOR HEALTHIER SEX

As given by Bay Area Physicians for Human Rights

NO RISK: *Most of these activities involve only skin-to-skin contact, thereby avoiding exposure to blood, semen, and vaginal secretions. This assumes there are no breaks in the skin.* 1) Social kissing (dry). 2) Body massage, hugging. 3) Body to body rubbing (frottage). 4) Light S&M (without bruising or bleeding). 5) Using one's own sex toys. 6) Mutual masturbation (male or external female). Care should be taken to avoid exposing the partners to ejaculate or vaginal secretions. Seminal, vaginal and salivary fluids should not be used as lubricants.

LOW RISK: *In these activities small amounts of certain body fluids might be exchanged, or the protective barrier might break causing some risk.* 1) **Anal or vaginal intercourse with condom.** Studies have shown that HIV does not penetrate the condom in simulated intercourse. Risk is incurred if the condom breaks or if semen spills into the rectum or vagina. The risk is further reduced if one withdraws before climax. 2) **Fellatio interruptus** (sucking, stopping before climax). Pre-ejaculate fluid may contain HIV. Saliva or other natural protective barriers in the mouth may inactivate virus in pre-ejaculate fluid. Saliva may contain HIV in low concentration. The insertive partner should warn the receptive partner before climax to prevent exposure to a large volume of semen. If mouth or genital sores are present, risk is increased. Likewise, action which causes mouth or genital injury will increase risk. 3) **Fellatio with condom** (sucking with condom) Since HIV cannot penetrate an intact condom, risk in this practice is very low unless breakage occurs. 4) **Mouth-to-mouth kissing** (French kissing, wet kissing) Studies have shown that HIV is present in saliva in such low concentration that salivary exchange is unlikely to transmit the virus. Risk is increased if sores in the mouth or bleeding gums are present. 5) **Oral-vaginal or oral-anal contact with protective barrier.** e.g. a latex dam, obtainable through a local dental supply house, may be used. Do not reuse latex barrier, because sides of the barrier may be reversed inadvertently. 6) **Manual anal contact with glove** (manual anal (fisting) or manual vaginal (internal) contact with glove). If the glove does not break, virus transmission should not occur. However, significant trauma can still be inflicted on the rectal tissues leading to other medical problems, such as hemorrhage or bowel perforation. 7) **Manual vaginal contact with glove** (internal). See above.

MODERATE RISK: *These activities involve tissue trauma and/or exchange of body fluids which may transmit HIV or other sexually transmitted disease.* 1) **Fellatio** (sucking to climax). Semen may contain high concentrations of HIV and if absorbed through open sores in the mouth or digestive tract could pose risk. 2) **Oral-anal contact** (rimming). HIV may be contained in blood-contaminated feces or in the anal rectal lining. This practice also poses high risk of transmission of parasites and other gastrointestinal infections. 3) **Cunnilingus** (oral-vaginal contact). Vaginal secretions and menstrual blood have been shown to harbor HIV, thereby causing risk to the oral partner if open lesions are present in the mouth or digestive tract. 4) **Manual rectal contact** (fisting). Studies have indicated a direct association between fisting and HIV infection for both partners. This association may be due to concurrent use of recreational drugs, bleeding, pre-fisting semen exposure, or anal intercourse with ejaculation. 5) **Sharing sex toys.** 6) **Ingestion of urine.** HIV has not been shown to be transmitted via urine; however, other immunosuppressive agents or infections may be transmitted in this manner.

HIGH RISK: *These activities have been shown to transmit HIV.* 1) **Receptive anal intercourse without condom.** All studies imply that this activity carries the highest risk of transmitting HIV. The rectal lining is thinner than that of the vagina or the mouth thereby permitting ready absorption of the virus from semen or pre-ejaculate fluid to the blood stream. One laboratory study suggests that the virus may enter by direct contact with rectal lining cells without any bleeding. 2) **Insertive anal intercourse without condom.** Studies suggest that men who participate only in this activity are at less risk of being infected than their partners who are rectally receptive; however the risk is still significant. It carries high risk of infection by other sexually transmitted diseases. 3) **Vaginal intercourse without condom.**